FIRST LIGHT

SHORT FICTION BY:

Alan Amrhine
Amy Bock
Robert Broomall
Sharon Broomall
T. L. Emery
Charles Godfrey
Bob Knapp
Joe Long
Keith Hoskins
Paul Sekulich
Mark Lee Taylor
Chris Vaughan

A Blue Stone Media Publication

Edited by Robert Broomall

BLUE STONE
M E D I A

ISBN-13: 978-0692417874
ISBN-10: 0692417877

Cover Photograph by Sharon Broomall
Cover Design by Alan Amrhine
www.bluestonemediapublishing.com

CONTENTS

Introduction

The short story is a unique art form, requiring discipline and tight writing. Because of the story's length, nine-tenths of it must, to paraphrase Hemingway, remain unsaid, and therein lies the craft of it. In the heyday of the pulps and of magazines like *Colliers* and the *Saturday Evening Post*, there was an extensive market for this kind of fiction. A good writer could make a living turning out nothing but shorts. Unfortunately, those days are long gone. Fortunately for us, though, writers are still doing short stories, and in *First Light*, Blue Stone Media presents a cross-section of the genre. There is something for everyone here, from Poe-like Gothic fantasy, to an old-fashioned detective story, to literary fiction. Even a Christmas story. And while many of these authors are unknown to the public now, we feel that won't be the case for long. We hope you enjoy this collection, the first in what we hope will become a series.

Robert Broomall

1937—Europe on the brink of war. Two men have the power to stop the impending catastrophe. Will they succeed? The secret is in . . .

THE BRIEFCASE

By Keith Hoskins

Frankfurt, Germany, Sachsenhausen District – 1937

Hans Dietrich looked at his pocket watch for the sixth time since entering the Donderbrauen Kneipe, a quaint tavern on the outskirts of Frankfurt. His contact wasn't late, but time was crucial; Dietrich was a wanted man, and quite possibly his country's last hope for a peaceful future.

From his small table in a quiet corner of the tavern, he looked around at the patrons and staff, making sure no one paid him any more attention than he deserved. He was just an old man, after all, drinking his schnapps and minding his own business. As far as they knew, he was here to enjoy a drink or two after a hard day's work. He lifted his glass and had a sip. Apples. *Is everything in this town made from apples?*

He looked around the bar and scrutinized the people again. Everyone seemed all right, minding their food and drink, sharing the latest gossip or news. The barman kept busy preparing for the evening rush, and the kellnerin who had waited on him occasionally glanced at his drink to see if it needed tending. Nothing more.

No, everyone was fine; no one seemed suspicious

or looked out of place. Dietrich postulated that the only one who fit that description here was himself. He hoped he wasn't that obvious. He was normally better at this sort of thing; he had done it a hundred times. But this was different; he wasn't meeting a fellow member or informant, the man he waited for was a stranger. He wasn't even German. But by the end of their conversation he would have to trust this man with, not only his life, but the lives of every citizen of Germany. Dietrich glanced around again; he had to be careful. The others were all dead, but he couldn't afford to die. Not just yet.

Dietrich looked to the chair to his right and at the large, brown leather briefcase that lay flat on the seat. It was a good briefcase; it had two strong straps that kept the case securely closed, and a large brass latch in the center that locked with a key. It had cost him sixty marks at the luggage store in Berlin. A bit expensive, but the price that had been paid for its contents was immeasurable.

Dietrich checked his watch: two minutes past four. Damn! Now he was late. *Where is he?* But, the man he was meeting was a doctor, and doctors were notorious for being late.

He'll be here. He'll show. Dietrich nodded to himself reassuringly.

The door opened and the cool, early May air seeped into the tavern. Although the calendar said spring, winter refused to let go. A tall, handsome man wearing a tan overcoat and matching hat walked in. He was about thirty-five years old, but he had a bit of old-soul look in his eyes. He wore brass trimmed glasses, and a billiard-style pipe hung from his mouth.

This could be the doctor; the description matched. He was alone, and he casually glanced around as if looking for someone. He stopped a kellnerin carrying a tray full of drinks and asked her a question. She pointed in Dietrich's general direction, and he walked over. Dietrich picked up a newspaper he had abandoned to the tabletop twenty minutes earlier and pretended to read the editor's column. The man placed his coat and hat on the rack off to the side, then took a seat at a small table adjacent to Dietrich's. He unfolded a newspaper of his own and, with the pipe still balanced in his mouth, he began to read.

Both men read their respective papers and now Dietrich had to make the next move.

"It's a beautiful day to go fishing," said Dietrich, not taking his nose from his open pages.

"It is," said the man, "but I prefer to do my fishing on the lake."

Both newspapers dropped. "Dr. Adler?" said Dietrich.

"Yes," replied the other. He stood and approached a chair opposite Dietrich. "May I?"

"Please."

Adler sat down, placed his pipe in his suit pocket, and folded his hands on the table. "One of my patients said you wanted to meet with me?" He smiled. Dietrich did not return the smile. This wasn't the time for pleasantries, but he knew he had to ease Adler into this. Too much too fast would certainly scare him off. "Something very important, she said," Adler added.

Adler's smile wasn't a nervous smile, but an appeasing one. One he had probably used many times to woo a woman, or calm a patient, or get a better price on a new watch. It was more of a politician's smile, and it was one he'd probably learned honestly.

"That would be an understatement, my good doctor. This will be the most important meeting of our lives. And I have had many important meetings."

"Really?" said Adler, his face now showing a well-rehearsed look of concern. "Well, you have my full attention, my good sir."

A kellnerin came over and placed her hand on Adler's shoulder. "And what can I get for you, mein herr?" asked the waitress. She wore a red and white dirndl with a green apron. Her golden hair framed a beautiful face and a bright smile.

"What do you recommend?" said Adler.

"Well, we are famous for our apfelwein. It is the best in Sachsenhausen."

"Then that's what I will have," said Adler, his politician's smile shining brightly.

The girl blushed, then turned to Dietrich. "And you, sir. Would you like another schnapps?"

Dietrich picked up the drink he had been nursing for the past hour, downed the remainder, and placed the empty glass on the table. "Please," he said to the waitress in a raspy voice as the alcohol drained down his throat. She grabbed his glass and headed back to the bar, but not before giving Adler a glancing grin.

As Adler gazed at the departing view of the waitress, Dietrich cleared his throat to get the doctor's attention back where it belonged. "If you are done flirting, Dr. Adler, we have urgent business that needs your complete attention."

"Right," said Adler, "the all-too important conversation." He furrowed his brow, feigning seriousness.

Dietrich frowned and shook his head. "I know men like you, Doctor. Just observing the world around them, but not willing to be a real participant when true action is required."

"With all due respect . . . I'm sorry, I don't even

know your name."

Dietrich hesitated. He normally wouldn't give up his name to a man he just met, but it didn't matter anymore. After tonight, his name might be all that would be left of him. Dietrich exhaled and answered. "Dietrich. Hans Dietrich."

"With all due respect, Herr Dietrich, you don't know me."

"I know more about you than you think," said Dietrich. "For one, you're a spy working for the American government."

"I assumed you knew that much since the patient who set up this meeting is one of my informants."

"I also know that you are an American citizen, and that you send monthly reports to the United States government on regular actions involving key Nazi personnel, up to and including Adolf Hitler."

"You've done your homework, Hans, but that doesn't—"

"Your reports go directly to Senator Henry Thomas, who just happens to be... your father."

Adler's jaw dropped a bit, stunned by Dietrich's revelation.

"Which brings me to your real name: Steven Thomas. You were born in West Chester, Pennsylvania, to the daughter of German immigrants. Her name was Hilda Adler, which is where you took your pseudo name from after you agreed to spy on my country at your father's behest. Growing up in a house with a German mother and grandparents, you learned the language and speak it almost flawlessly. You are a real doctor, and you received your degree from Harvard Medical School. Currently, you have a wife and two sons living in Chevy Chase, Maryland. How is that, Doctor? Do I now know you sufficiently?"

"How the hell—" Adler cut himself off as the kellnerin returned with their drinks.

"Here you are, meine herren." She placed the glasses on the table. "Is there anything else I can get for you?" Although she spoke to both men, her eyes flicked to Adler, who was too rattled by Dietrich's revelations to pursue any more flirtatious activity and barely gave the waitress a look in return.

"That will be all for now, fraulein," said Dietrich. "Thank you."

Adler waited until the kellnerin was out of earshot before he said, "Who the hell are you, Hans?"

It was Dietrich's turn to smile. Now, he had the man's attention. "Dr. Adler, have you ever heard of the Widerstand?"

"Yes. It's an alleged underground organization that is attempting to undermine the current government in Germany."

"There is nothing alleged about it. There are dozens of cells all around Germany, all operating independently. I should know; I was the organizer of one of those cells. And now, I am its last surviving member."

"The rest of your cell is dead?"

"Murdered," said Dietrich with venom in his voice. "We were about to complete our task of stopping the Nazi regime when we were hunted down by the Gestapo and executed by their SS monsters."

"Stop the Nazi regime from what?"

"From plunging Germany into another great war, Herr Doctor."

"Another great war?" Adler asked in surprise and took a sip of his apple wine. "Isn't Germany still licking its wounds from the last one? Besides, the Treaty of Versailles—"

"The Treaty of Versailles was a slap in the face to Germany. Adolph Hitler and his followers plan to make everyone responsible pay for the harsh penalties laid upon us." Dietrich stared at his schnapps then back at Adler. "Many of us citizens do not want to see our beloved country go to the brink of annihilation and thousands of her countrymen killed for the ideology of a few madmen."

"I don't think you have anything to worry about, Herr Dietrich. The rest of Europe—the rest of the world won't let that happen again."

"But it is happening, Doctor Adler. In all the reports you've sent to your father, you have to have seen the signs that Hitler is building his Army and the retaking of former German lands."

"We know about the conscription of the people for the Army, and we were surprised, but not too concerned, about the reoccupation of the Rhineland. Many of our statesmen believe that is France's fault."

"You mean France's problem," Dietrich corrected. Adler gave him a half smile. "Believe me, Doctor, those things you mentioned are just the beginning." Dietrich motioned to the chair next to him. "In this briefcase is a two-year collection of information showing that the Nazi party has plans to have Germany 'claim that which is rightfully hers,' to use the words of Hitler himself."

Adler glanced at the briefcase. "So, you have a few notes on the Nazis complaining about how unfair the treaty was. Everyone knows how they feel, and everyone knows Hitler isn't bold enough to start an all-out war with Europe. My informants and contacts have shown me no evidence that anything serious is stirring in Berlin."

"With all due respect, Doctor, but I believe you

and your colleagues are being naive. As well, I'm sure you have been intentionally fed disinformation by your so-called informants. Inside the briefcase are documents, photographs, recordings, and letters from and to Hitler himself. All of it showing plans for the expansion of Germany and the purification of its people."

"Purification?"

"Yes, Doctor. Every Jew, homosexual, and communist will be targeted; essentially anyone who is not of pure German descent and who is not a true representative of its people."

"We are well aware of the Nuremburg Laws stripping the Jews of all their rights, but you make it sound like Hitler wants to eradicate these people. What's he going to do, have them lined up and shot in the streets?"

"It may be just that simple." Dietrich took a drink of his schnapps. "The details are in the briefcase."

"And what of this 'expansion of Germany'? I assume that means he wants to take back more of the land Germany lost in the treaty."

"That and more. By this time next year, Austria could very well be an annexed state of the Third Reich."

"Austria?"

"Yes. And then Czechoslovakia, and then possibly Poland. In fact, Hitler is meeting with Stalin next month to discuss a possible invasion of Poland. A photograph of a letter to him from Hitler is in the briefcase. In fact, a copy of Hitler's itinerary for the entire months of May and June is in there as well."

"Do you realize what you're saying?" Adler said. "If Germany puts one soldier into any of those countries, the treaty would be broken and would cause..." Adler paused as the realization hit him.

"It would cause war, my good Doctor." Dietrich nodded, knowing Adler had finally caught on. "It would thrust Germany into another massive war with Europe."

It was Adler's turn to take a drink from his glass, and he managed to down its entire contents in one gulp.

The tavern door swung open with harsher than normal force. Three men in long gray overcoats walked in, followed by two men in black uniforms. The men in the gray overcoats spread out through the bar while the uniformed men stood guard by the door.

The men in gray had the swagger of men who had no fear. Why should they? When you are above the law and have the power of judge, jury, and executioner, you bestow fear, you don't experience it. Such was the existence of agents of the secret police.

"Gestapo," Dietrich whispered to Adler, who was himself carefully watching the men.

"And SS," said Adler. Dietrich noticed the distinctive insignias on the collars of the black-uniformed men. Adler was right.

"Why are they here?" Adler asked rhetorically.

"They are looking for me," Dietrich said matter-of-factly. Adler shot him a look.

"They followed you here?" a bit of panic was in Adler's voice.

"Most likely doing random searches. They may know I'm in Frankfurt. They shouldn't have a picture of me, and I'm almost certain that my fellow members wouldn't have divulged my identity to them."

"Almost?"

Dietrich shrugged. "That depends on how *persuasive* the Gestapo was in their questioning."

The three Gestapo agents had split up and were working their way around the establishment questioning patrons and employees. Dietrich could see fear in the people's wide eyes. Although they knew nothing about the resistance cells, they all feared the Gestapo and the free-rein, ruthless rule they had over the populace.

"What do we do?" asked Adler. He was a bit more nervous but otherwise kept his composure.

"We do nothing, Doctor Adler. We are simply two men having a drink on a Monday afternoon."

It took no time for one of the Gestapo agents to make his way to Dietrich's and Adler's table. He made a casual, but purposeful, beeline straight for them.

"Guten tag, meine herren. May I ask what you gentlemen are doing here in Sachsenhausen this fine afternoon?" The agent was young, maybe a few years younger than Adler. He had straight blond hair, and he beamed with confidence. He was probably one of Hitler's fine examples of the perfect German citizen.

"We are merely having a few drinks at the end of a hard day," replied Dietrich.

"I see. May I see your papers, please?"

Dietrich and Adler both reached for the inside pockets of their jackets and handed their identification papers to the Gestapo agent. He opened Adler's first.

"It says you are a doctor, Herr Adler."

"Yes," replied Adler and signaled the waitress for another drink.

"And your practice and residence are both in Berlin," continued the agent. "Why are you so far from home, Doctor?"

Dietrich couldn't let Adler ruin this whole operation, so he interjected. "He came to see me—"

"I was addressing the doctor," said the agent with a scowl and condescending tone. "When I want answers from you, I will address you."

Dietrich nodded and grabbed his glass.

"I am waiting for an answer, Herr Doctor."

Adler swallowed, inhaled, and answered. "My main practice is in Berlin; however, I have a second office in Frankfurt to accommodate my patients who live in the south."

"I see," said the agent. "And what is the address of that Frankfurt office?"

"24659 Schillerstraub."

"And you, Herr Dietrich, it says here that you are a cabinet maker in Dusseldorf. What are you doing in Frankfurt?"

"To see Doctor Adler. I'm a patient of his."

"Do they not have doctors in Dusseldorf?" the agent asked as he continued inspecting the identification papers.

"Yes, but Doctor Adler came highly recommended. You see I have—"

"Recommended by whom?"

"A friend. He said Doctor Adler was—"

"Name?"

The barrage of questions was an attempt to get Dietrich to slip up in a lie. An old but effective trick. Fortunately, Dietrich was too good for that; he had perfected the befuddled old man routine years ago. "My name? I thought you knew my name. Isn't it on my papers?"

"Not your name, your friend's name."

"I have many friends. Which—"

"The friend that recommended Doctor Adler."

"Oh, that would be Fritz Zimmer. He's a longtime customer of mine."

"And if you are seeing Doctor Adler as a patient, why are you here in this tavern with him?"

"You don't like this tavern?" Dietrich asked innocently.

"At the moment, Herr Dietrich, I don't like you. Now, tell me, why are the two of you here?"

"To have a drink, of course," Dietrich said as he raised his glass and gave a very toothy grin. The Gestapo agent looked from Dietrich to Adler. He was obviously frustrated from talking with the old man and on the verge of releasing his anger.

"He insisted on treating me to a drink," Adler said in response to the agent's glare.

"For being such a great doctor!" Dietrich said. He then he took his schnapps, threw it down his throat, and placed the empty glass back on the table just a little too hard so that it clumsily fell over.

"Do you normally have drinks with your patients, Doctor?"

"No, but Herr Dietrich wouldn't take no for an answer." Adler gave Dietrich a concerned look. He probably thought they were pushing their luck with the Gestapo agent, but Dietrich knew that lying to the Gestapo was a unique skill that had to be done convincingly.

The Gestapo agent looked at Dietrich, suspicion lingered in his eyes. Dietrich did his best not to make eye contact with him. A well-trained agent could read a man by deciphering his eyes.

"I think your *patient* has had one too many drinks, Herr Doctor. Make sure he finds his way home."

"I will," Adler replied.

The agent closed their identification booklets, placed them on the table, and walked back towards the door where the other two agents waited. The kellnerin brought Adler his drink; she must have been waiting for the agent to leave before she approached the men's table. Dietrich was ready to breathe a sigh of relief until the agent turned around in mid-stride.

"So, whose idea was it to come here?"

"Pardon?" said Adler who was started at the agent's return.

"This tavern," said the agent as he waved his arm to gesture the entirety of the place. "Whose idea was it to come to this particular establishment?"

"It was mine," replied Adler.

"And why did you pick this place?"

"For the apfelwein, of course," he said, raising his glass. "It is the best in Sachsenhausen."

"Yes," said the agent, forcing a smile. "So I've heard." He was about to turn around again when he noticed the briefcase sitting on the chair. "That is a nice briefcase, Herr Dietrich."

"Actually," said Adler, "it's mine. It's a bit too big for my use. It cost me fifty marks in Berlin. It's yours for forty." The agent gave Adler a stone-faced look. "Thirty-five, then?" The Gestapo agent looked to Dietrich and then to Adler and then back to the briefcase. His eyes focused on it for what seemed an eternity.

"Guten tag, meine herren." The agent turned and joined his fellow Gestapo; together with the SS officers, they left the Donderbrauen Kneipe.

"That was too close," said Dietrich, then he motioned to the kellnerin for another schnapps. Adler grabbed his apple wine and drank it slowly until his hands stopped shaking. He placed the glass down and gave Dietrich a stern look.

"What are you trying to get me into, Dietrich?" Adler was visibly angry, and Dietrich couldn't blame him.

"I'm sorry, Doctor Adler, but—"

"Sorry?" Adler said at a slightly elevated volume. He looked around to see if he caught anyone's attention and then continued in a voice of more discretion. "You bring me here all the way from Berlin, tell me a tale of exaggerated fears about unfathomable deeds that most likely won't happen, and then the damn Gestapo and SS come in and interrogate us here in our seats." Adler grabbed his wine again and drank the remainder in the glass.

"Believe me, Doctor, that was hardly an interrogation. If they had suspected that either of us was with the Widerstand we would be in the back of one of their cars heading off to meet our end, but not before they did everything they could to get as much information out of us as possible."

"What do you want from me, Hans?" said Adler with a bit of exasperation. "I may be a spy, but I am very low level. I'm not much more than a glorified messenger."

"Right now, that's exactly what I want. I need— Germany needs— you to take this briefcase to your father in America. He needs to see the truth behind all our 'exaggerated fears' as you call them. And then he must share that knowledge with his fellow senators."

"I can send it to him via my standard—"

"No," Dietrich interrupted. "*You* must take it to him. It must be hand delivered by someone he and I both trust, someone who can vouch for its contents."

"I can't vouch for anything that's in there," said Adler. "I don't know where any of it came from. And, how do I know *you* aren't trying to give me and the United States disinformation?"

Dietrich sighed and took off his glasses. He rubbed the ridge of his nose, cleaned the lenses with a handkerchief, and then put the glasses back on. "I know this is a lot to take in, Doctor Adler, but I need you to have faith in me. Dozens of people have died getting the information in that briefcase. Good people; friends and good, honest citizens. We love our country, Doctor, but we don't like where our Fuhrer is taking us. We need to show the world what is happening so they can help us before it becomes too late."

"Why me?" asked Adler. "Why the United States? Why not France or England?"

"If Hitler begins his conquest of Europe, France and England will not be prepared for him. The United States will, once again, ignore what is happening over here, and hope that it goes away. We need them to intervene before Hitler becomes too powerful. We need the Allied forces that banded together twenty years ago to do so again; this time not to fight a war, but to prevent one."

"And you have real proof that war is inevitable?" Adler asked.

"In here," Dietrich said as he placed his hand on the briefcase. "Everything is in here. The proof is irrefutable. And as far as the authenticity of it goes, I'm sure your nation's government has highly competent individuals who can verify that the items in here are very real and quite damning."

Adler sat there digesting all that Dietrich had told him. After a minute of silence he said, "Why me?"

"As I said, we need someone of notoriety to hand deliver this information."

"No, it seems that you are coming to me rather hastily on this; things seem rushed and desperate."

"Very true, Doctor. Two nights ago, the man we had arranged to take this briefcase to the United States was killed. He was the unfortunate victim of an automobile accident."

"I take it that you don't believe it was an accident."

"Not for a minute. After his 'accident,' our group members were hunted down one by one until only I remained. There is no question that we had been revealed by a traitor in our midst. Fortunately, I was the one in charge of meeting our courier and giving him this briefcase. Also, fortunately, I was aware of you and who you are. You seemed like the most logical choice to replace our fallen man."

"How was this courier going to get this package to America? Who was he?"

"Are you familiar with Jonathan Bishop?"

"The ambassador's aide?" Adler's eyes went wide with realization. "Jon Bishop, the aide to the American ambassador to Germany, was your delivery man?"

"Yes. And now that task must fall onto you."

"And if I refuse?" asked Adler.

"Then we have no hope of stopping Adolph Hitler." Dietrich raised his empty glass to signal the kellnerin that he needed a fresh schnapps. Then, to Adler he said: "Besides, Doctor, it may be too late for you to say no."

"What do you mean?"

"I will most likely be caught and killed just like my fellow members, and when they do catch me, they will find all the people I have had contact with over the past couple days. That means they will find out that I have been to this tavern and that I was talking with you."

"No one could know th—" Adler paused as the afternoon's events came crashing upon him in a shower of reality. "The Gestapo agent."

"Exactly," said Dietrich.

The kellnerin came with two bottles in her hands. One was the schnapps for Dietrich, the other was a carafe of what appeared to be apple wine for Adler. "More schnapps?" Dietrich nodded and the waitress poured. "And you, mein herr?" Adler nodded slightly as he stared blankly at the table. She filled his wine glass and left the two men alone.

Dietrich sipped his schnapps and stared at Adler. This was a lot for the doctor to accept in one night, but he seemed like a decent man and he would make the right decision. At least, Dietrich hoped so. But Adler was an American, and Americans cared for nothing save their own selfish lives. Living so far away, the problems of Europe were nothing more than stories. And if Adolph Hitler became the monster that Dietrich feared, then America would see him as just another one of Europe's problems. Adler needed to be different; he needed to be the man he hoped—

"I'll do it," said Adler, still looking at the table. He slowly raised his gaze and looked into Dietrich's eyes. "I'll deliver the briefcase to my father."

Dietrich smiled; a smile of happiness, a smile of relief. "Thank you, Herr Doctor. You will be our savior." He reached across the table and grasped Adler's folded hands. "You have my and my country's eternal gratitude."

Adler forced a smile. Dietrich could tell that he was still a bit unsure and probably a bit scared. Good. That would keep him on his toes and possibly alive.

"I assume you have a plan for getting me home," said Adler. "To America, that is."

Dietrich reached into his inside pocket once more and removed an envelope and placed it on the table. "In here is the key to the briefcase as well as a ticket for a ship that will go directly to the United States." Dietrich paused and stared at the envelope. "This was supposed to be Bishop's ticket."

"I understand," Adler nodded. "When does the ship leave?"

"Tonight at seven o'clock."

"Tonight? Seven?" Panic was in Adler's voice. "I need to go home and pack. I have patients to see tomorrow. I need to call—"

"There is no time for that, Doctor. You must leave here and go straight to the ship."

Adler looked at his watch. "But, I'll never make the docks in two hours."

Dietrich gave Adler a reassuring smile. "It's not that kind of ship, Doctor."

Adler frowned and gave Dietrich a puzzled look. Dietrich pushed the envelope toward Adler. "Welcome to the resistance." He then raised his glass and toasted his new recruit. "Prost!"

"Prost!" Adler returned the salute with his own glass, then the two men drank.

"It really is good apfelwein," Adler admitted.

"The best in Sachsenhausen," Dietrich added.

They both smiled.

Adler put down his glass and looked at the briefcase. It sat there like a punished child, waiting for one of its parents to rescue it from its place of abandonment. Was Adler ready for this responsibility? Dietrich prayed he was; he was their only hope. Dietrich needed to have faith in Adler just as Dietrich needed Adler to have faith in him.

"You will have three days before you reach America; take that time to look through the briefcase and really look at what we have accomplished. Look at all the information, and then you will truly believe all that I have said here this afternoon."

"I will," said Adler. "I promise." He then picked up the envelope that sat so ominously in front of him. He opened it, removed the key, and placed it in his breast pocket. He removed the ticket, read it, and smiled.

"Something amusing, Herr Doctor?" asked Dietrich.

"There is one good thing about this mission."

"And what is that?"

"I've always wanted to ride on the *Hindenburg*."

Here's an old-fashioned mystery, old-fashioned except for the fact that it's set in outer space...

THE BRIDE

By Chris Vaughan

Curt Baniker didn't smile often, but when Kate Quinlan's daughter walked into the office of his detective agency, it was like he'd stepped back thirty years. She was her mother's spitting image, from her ultramarine eyes down to her dimpled knees.

She returned his smile so warmly he felt a little pang in his heart—perhaps a last ember from the torch he'd carried for her mother. "You must be Mr. Baniker." Even her voice was like Kate's.

Baniker realized he was standing, although he couldn't remember getting up. He squeezed around his desk, which filled the austere room, and took her by the hand. "Please, call me Curt. You look just like your mother, Ms. Quinlan."

"I get that a lot," she said. "I'm Lucy."

"Lucy." He liked it. He gestured to one of the two chairs in front of his desk. "Have a seat."

Lucy sat down and crossed her long legs. She was wearing a short dress that rode high on her thighs, and Baniker felt the stirring of feelings best left buried with the anatomy that had been buried with them. He'd been decimated by a concussion bomb during the Martian rebellion, and what remained of the man was deeply scarred.

Baniker made his way stiffly back around his desk, and by the time he settled back into his seat even the memory of the smile was gone from his

20

face. He decided not to ask after Lucy's mother just then. "What brings you to Sun City, Lucy?"

Sun City was the colloquial name for Mercury Station, the largest spaceport in the inner system. It orbited the sun in the protection of Mercury's shadow, and hosted millions of travelers and tourists every day. This was in addition to its more than ten million permanent residents, of whom Baniker was one.

"I'm here to get married," Lucy said.

"Congratulations," he said, trying not to sound bitter.

"Thank you," Lucy said. "We're scheduled for tomorrow at 12:30 at the Starburst Chapel."

The Starburst Chapel was located at the only point on the station where the sun—or, at least, its corona—was visible. It cost a fortune to reserve, and yet it was booked up years in advance. Lucy or her fiancé had money. "I hope you get to see a flare."

Lucy beamed.

"What can I do for you?"

Her smile evaporated, and she glanced around nervously. "This *is* confidential, isn't it?"

"Initial consultations are privileged, and I use the best jammers available, so we won't be overheard."

"I'm sorry, it's just that I'm here for my fiancé, and there are a lot of people who'd love to... Well, he's Linus Kellerman."

Baniker leaned forward. "The Arch-Bishop of Sacramento's son?"

Lucy nodded. "The same."

Bishop Kellerman was one of the richest and most powerful men alive. His Church of the Prosperous Interpretation had adherents in every nation, every colony, every outpost. He dined with Emperors and advised Oligarchs.

His son, by contrast, was a regular in the tablogs. They called him "Luscious Linus." He was one of the worlds' most eligible bachelors, but he was more notorious for a long string of torrid affairs and bad decisions.

"He doesn't know I'm here. He doesn't even know I know. I overheard him and the Bishop talking." She paused and took a breath. "He's being blackmailed."

"By who?"

"A little weasel named Arnie Carr."

Baniker used the interface on his desk to bring up Carr's criminal record. It projected his mug shots and rap sheet above the desk. "He's a shifty looking scuzzer all right. Petty theft, possession, smuggling contraband. Nothing major—lucky for him. He gets caught a lot."

"You can add blackmail to that list," Lucy said.

"He has to get caught first." Baniker minimized the display. "What's he got on Linus?"

"As you probably know, Linus made some bad choices when he was younger—before I met him. He's a good man—he always has been—but he had all that fame and money and no guidance. The Bishop was always too busy for Linus."

Poor little rich kid, Baniker thought.

Lucy looked down. "He was dealing Damage."

Damage was one of the latest designer drugs. Its name came from the abbreviation for its chemical formula: D.M.G. Baniker couldn't pronounce the actual name of the drug, but he'd seen its effects first hand. It came in colorful little pills that could send a user on a wild hallucinogenic trip, or put him into a coma. It was unpredictable, and it could be deadly. Mostly wealthy kids used it, which was why almost every government had severe penalties for trafficking in the drug.

"That's pretty serious," Baniker said. "What does Carr have on him?"

"I don't know exactly. Carr was one of Linus' distributors, so it could be anything," Lucy said. "I overheard something about vids."

"Why come to me? It sounds like Linus already went to his father. Surely the old man has people for this kind of thing."

"The Bishop paid Arnie's fee—two million credits—and now he considers the matter closed."

"He paid Arnie off?" Baniker was surprised. Even if Arnie had vids showing Linus taking money for Damage, it still wouldn't be enough to prove he'd been a dealer. With his connections and resources, the Bishop should have lawyered up. At worst, his son might get a hefty fine and time served. Whatever evidence Carr had, it must have been damning. "Did they get the evidence?"

"I don't know. All I know is that the Bishop is furious with Linus. If Arnie asks for more, the Bishop will personally turn Linus in to save face."

Baniker did a cursory search for Linus's criminal record but couldn't find one. That was no small feat given the boy's history in the rags. If not for his powerful father, Baniker suspected Linus would be doing hard labor in Peru, or sweeping out exhaust vents on Mexican freighters. "It looks like his father's been looking out for him pretty good so far. If Carr comes back for more, he'll just pony up again. It's not like he doesn't have the credits." Or make Carr disappear, Baniker thought. That's what kings did, and Kellerman was a king in every way that mattered except name.

Lucy's eyes welled up. A single tear spilled over and traced a trail down her cheek. "Maybe you're right," she said.

Baniker looked away. Anywhere but those

damned eyes. Something wasn't adding up. Why had they paid Carr when they had so many better options? "When did they pay him?"

"Two weeks ago."

"It hasn't been long enough to know what Carr will do, but I think you're right. He'll be back as soon as he burns through the two million credits."

Lucy wiped the tear from her cheek and smiled. "You'll help me?"

Baniker sighed. There was no percentage in it. The last thing he needed was a rich and powerful enemy, and—if Baniker succeeded in getting the evidence from Carr—that's exactly what he'd have in Kellerman. Not Linus—the Bishop. Whatever evidence Carr had, the old man was willing to pay to suppress it—and it was harder than getting ice out of the Sun than it was to get money from a Prosperitarian. And who'd he be helping? Linus? That ass was only breathing free air because of an accident of birth. By rights, the Damage-pusher should be wife to some fat Yankee smuggler in an Australian penal colony.

"He's a good person," Lucy said. "He deserves a second chance."

Baniker guessed that whatever chance Linus was on, it was way past his second, but—God—she looked like her mother.

Kate Quinlan had been an engineer aboard Baniker's first ship, the *ISS Penelope*. He'd fallen in love with her the first time he'd seen her—which must have amused the worldly and beautiful woman to no end, but she'd protected his heart and nurtured his childish crush into true friendship. He would do anything for Kate.

"My mother said you would help me," Lucy said.

"I'm going to regret this."

***

"Why are you looking into this Carr guy, anyway?" Mike Quayle had been Baniker's partner during his last few years on station security. Now he was Baniker's back door into the station's vast law-enforcement resources. He was also a friend, or as close to being one as Baniker allowed.

They were in Jeter's, a dive bar near Quayle's duty station, and Baniker had to strain to hear over the ambient noise of Klunk music and drunken conversations. Finding Carr had been surprisingly easy. The weasel was running a delivery service, using an aging packet ship he'd bought at auction.

"Does it matter?" Baniker said.

"Yeah."

"Too bad, it's confidential."

"So's this data," Quayle snapped.

"How confidential are flight plans and ships' manifests?"

"Confidential enough that you can't get them without my help." Quayle shrugged and handed Baniker a datapad under the table. "Aw, who cares? The sack of shit is working for the Americans."

"As if I didn't hate this guy enough," Baniker said. He opened the pad's display. "Does it say what he's running?"

"All kinds of legit merchandise. Squeaky, in fact."

"You know what that means," Baniker said.

"Dirty as a boomer's jumper, Sarge."

Baniker brought up Carr's flight plans for the last two standard years. A gridwork of red lines appeared on the pad with the inner Solar System's major bodies arrayed across it using N14 projection—a fourteen-dimensional system of algorithms that allowed interplanetary routes to be laid out in straight paths on a two-dimensional grid regardless of planetary positions over time. The math was beyond anyone lacking an advanced degree, but it worked like a charm.

"Look at that," Baniker said. All of the courses intersected the same small patch of space near Venus.

"That's just about dead smack in the middle of nowhere," Quayle said as he looked over Baniker's shoulder. "Why would a greasy little scuzzer like Carr go there so often?"

"Looks like he's going to be there in seventeen hours," Baniker said, looking at Carr's current flight plan. "I can be there in eight. That's some coincidence."

"You don't believe in coincidences?" Quayle said.

"You're right, I don't."

It seemed like a quick run to Venus was in Baniker's future. He checked Carr's flight plans again. The creep had been running non-stop for the last eighteen months. At least that gave Baniker a good idea where Carr was keeping whatever evidence he had on Linus Kellerman.

***

Arnie Carr eased his packet ship into orbital velocity, triggering a flashing red alarm light on the console. He ignored it. The damn "check engine" light came on every time he dropped below two-thousand meters per second, but he wasn't about to sink another blessed credit into this aging P.O.S. His eye twitched.

Venus's white profile dominated the starboard half of his viewport. The hula-girl suctioned to the top of the console was a dancing silhouette against it. *Sometimes space is so damn beautiful,* Carr thought.

The proximity alarm went off. Carr stabbed its kill switch with a greasy finger and checked the scanners. A second ship—slightly larger than his own—was moving to intercept him. "Come on, already, I've got a tight schedule."

After a few long moments, a voice crackled over his radio. "That you, Blackbird?"

"Who the hell else would it be?" Carr muttered. He grabbed the microphone and pressed the transmit button. "It's me. Let's get this over with—I'm due at Lory in twelve hours."

"What's the good word, Blackbird?"

Carr rolled his eyes. These guys were such amateurs. "Blessed are the industrious, for they prepare the way."

"Confirmed, Blackbird. Prepare for docking."

Carr replaced the microphone. "Prepare for docking," he said mockingly. His eye twitched.

The proximity alarm sounded again, sending Carr's heart racing.

"Yeah, yeah, I know," Carr barked as he hit the kill button a second time. He was uttering a string of angry profanities when he saw the scanner display. The words died in his throat. There was a new blip—a big one—coming in fast behind Carr's co-conspirators. It's transponder identified it as a Pacifican gunship—more than twice his size and armed to the teeth.

His hand shook as he laid in a course away from the rendezvous. "You pig farmers are on your own," he said to the otherwise empty cabin as he powered up the fusion drive.

Something hit his ship. It shuddered so hard his teeth clacked together, and then the rising hum of the reactor dropped away to nothing.

"No!"

A voice boomed over his radio. "Attention, unidentified vessel, you have been disabled. Stand down and prepare to be boarded."

Carr grabbed the microphone. He hadn't taken on any of the contraband yet, so all he had was a hold full of legit cargo. They had nothing on him but an unsubstantiated opinion. "Why are you shooting at me? I'm a law-abiding citizen, scuzzhead!"

Before the Pacificans could respond, there was a bright light above his ship, and Carr watched as his co-conspirators made a run for it. There was a second flash a moment later as the gun ship launched after them.

"Ha! Give 'em a good run for their money, boys!"

Carr's happiness was short lived. His engines were trashed. He wasn't going anywhere. All he could do was sit and wait for the Pacificans to come back. By then, the morons on the other ship would have given him up. His eye twitched.

***

Carr was shivering even though he was wrapped in two blankets. Without the engines, his ship was cooling fast. If the authorities didn't come back soon, he'd freeze to death.

The proximity alarm bleeped to life.

"Finally," Carr said.

"Attention packet ship, this is the Gibsonian freighter *Lorenzo*. Do you need assistance?"

Carr couldn't believe his luck. The Gibsonians were religious kooks who saw themselves as the Good Samaritans of the spaceways. They'd help him just because they thought God would want them to. Hell, they'd even shelter him from the authorities. They were nothing like the opportunistic, money-grubbing Prosperity prigs. He grabbed the microphone. "Affirmative, *Lorenzo*. I could use a tow, boys."

There was a long delay. Then, "Negative. We don't have the fuel. Just enough to get to port. We can send back help."

Carr's eye twitched. He couldn't believe his ears, he'd be an ice cube by the time anyone could reach him. He should have radioed for help hours ago, but he'd been praying for a miracle, and here it was—only his saviors were idiots. "How about a lift, then, *Lorenzo*? My life support's down."

There was a shorter delay. "Can do, friend, but we're packed to the stays. No luggage, and you still might have to hold your breath part of the way."

These amateurs were cutting it close with their fuel. Carr was amazed they were willing to help him. He would lose his cargo—the Americans would make him pay for it, plus a scuzzload of interest—but maybe he could avoid jail time.

Carr overrode the engine safeguards while *Lorenzo* completed its docking maneuvers. He programmed a forced restart in thirty minutes that would inject the ship's entire remaining fuel supply directly into the damaged plenum. The old packet ship would blow to Kingdom Come, and the Pacificans would think their shots had caused the explosion. They'd figure Carr had been killed in the explosion, and he'd be free to rebuild. With his golden ticket, that wouldn't take long.

Maybe he wouldn't even bother to rebuild. There were still a lot of nice places a man like Carr could retire. Tahiti was getting a little crowded, but he'd heard Tobago was nice. Carr cackled as he popped the hula girl from the console and stuffed her into the folds of his shirt. Then he headed back to the airlock.

When he opened the hatch, a powerful arm

grabbed him by his collar and pulled him through into a small airlock on the *Lorenzo*. The big ape who owned the arm pushed Carr out of the way and sealed the hatch.

"We'd better get out of here, fast," Carr said. The big man turned to face him and Carr's throat went dry. Deep scars covered the left side of the man's face. "You ain't no Gibsonian," Carr said. His eye twitched.

The big man tore the hula girl from Carr's shirt and broke it open with his bare hands. "What'd you bring with you?"

"Hey, that's mine, you farking space ape."

The big man shook the parts of the doll and then dropped them onto the deck. "What else do you have?"

"Nothin'. What is this, a shakedown? You told me not to bring nothin'."

The big man was even stronger than he looked. He spun Carr around and frisked him, and all Carr could do was gasp. When he didn't find whatever it was he was looking for, the big man opened the inside door of the airlock and pushed Carr through into an empty cargo hold.

"You said you didn't have any room."

The big man jabbed Carr in the chest. "I don't have room for your shit, Carr."

"You know who I am?"

"Take your clothes off. Now."

Carr's eye twitched. "That's not the kind of ride I wanted."

"Shut up and strip."

"I got rights," Carr said. "You're a cop, ain't ya?"

The big man grabbed Carr by his shirt and slammed him against the bulkhead. Carr's feet dangled above the deck. "You've got nothing, Carr. If you don't want me to toss you out that airlock, you'd better shut up and do what you're told."

"Okay, okay. Take it easy."

The big man dropped him and Carr started to disrobe. "Just take it easy on me, okay? My ass is virgin."

The big man ignored him. Instead, he rooted through Carr's clothes as soon as Carr took them off. After that proved fruitless, he made Carr bend over and cough.

"I knew you were a cop," Carr said. "None of you can resist looking at assholes. Who gave you that face? Wish he'd finished the job."

The big man's face clouded over and he took a menacing step toward Carr. For a moment, Carr thought he was done for, but, to his relief, the big man turned away and took a portable medical scanner from a storage closet.

The big man ran the scanner over Carr, grunted, and scanned Carr again. "Where is it? I know you wouldn't have left it on the ship."

"Left what? Look, Magilla, I gotta tell you—in about ten minutes my ship's gonna blow sky high. Whatever it is you're after, you ain't gonna get it if your ship's still attached when it does."

***

"He torched his ship?" Quayle was talking to Baniker from a private room on the Pacifican gun ship. Baniker was sitting in *Lorenzo's* command module, feeling more than a little frustrated. Quayle said, "I hope you got what you wanted first."

Baniker hadn't found the evidence yet, but he was positive that Carr had it with him on his ship, and that had he brought it with him somehow. Carr wasn't the trusting type, and Baniker figured the evidence was worth billions. There was no way that little scuzzer would risk letting it out of his hands.

Baniker was missing something. "What'd you learn about the guys in the other ship?" he asked Quayle.

"They're nobodies. A couple of errand boys—they work at a mission on Phobos. They say that once every standard month or so they rendezvous with a ship near their outpost, take on a load of drugs, and then transport it to Venus, where they meet up with—met up—with Carr. They didn't know who he was. Called him 'Blackbird.'"

"How'd they know when to pick up a shipment?"

"They got coded messages disguised as letters from home. We'll look into them, but they'll be untraceable."

"Wait. Did you say they were working at a mission?" Baniker frowned. Was this another coincidence? "You mean like a church mission?"

"I suppose, why?"

Baniker ran a search for missions on Phobos. He wasn't surprised when only one came up—the Martian moon was one of the most desolate outposts in the system. In fact, there really wasn't much logic in putting a mission on Phobos unless it wasn't the souls of your fellow man you were worried about. That was why Baniker was even less surprised when the Church of the Prosperous Interpretation came up as its sponsor.

The last piece snapped into place.

"You ready to hand over Carr?" Quayle asked.

"I need a little more time."

"Look, Sarge, I can't sit out here waiting forever. You've got no idea how many regs I'm breaking for you."

"One more hour. Then he'll be all yours."

"You'll owe me big."

"You'll get credit for this collar, won't you?"

Quayle blew out an exasperated breath. "Okay—one more hour—but that's it. You've got some nerve."

Baniker smiled.

"Christ, you're an ugly bastard when you smile, Sarge."

Baniker cut the connection.

***

"I see you're a big fan of Malevich."

"Who?" Carr's eye twitched.

"The Russian neuroscientist?"

"I still don't understand."

Baniker waited. Carr watched him, wide eyed. Then he twitched again.

"There!" Baniker pointed at Carr's face.

"What?"

"That tic. It started around the same time you started putting encoded information into your mitochondrial DNA."

"You're farking insane."

"Malevich was the first to theorize that information could be encoded in the inactive portions of mitochondrial DNA. Your body has the ability to detect and repair damaged nuclear DNA, but this process isn't as robust in mitochondrial DNA. The repair can be retarded and even prevented by a number of drugs. Malevich hit on the idea because nerve cells are the longest lived cells in the human body, so that made them the logical containers for modified DNA. Once cells die, the information is cleaned up along with the other inert tissue from the dead cell. You don't want your data cells dying."

Baniker opened the door to the medical cabinet.

"My ship's going to explode any minute," Carr

said.

Baniker said, "The big problem with using nerve cells – well, one of the two big problems, really—is that mitrochondria are integral to the transmission of signals along your nerves." Baniker found a nano-needle in the cabinet. "If you screw with them, you get things—like tics."

Carr's eye twitched, and Baniker pointed at it with the needle. "That's what we call a 'tell.' "

Carr pressed on his eyelid.

"You know the second big problem with using nerve-cell mitochondrial DNA for storing data?"

Carr nodded.

"That's right, it hurts like a bitch coming out."

***

The news covered the net by noon: *Prosperity Kingpin: Bishop Kellerman Running Massive Damage Ring*. An empire was toppling. Clips of government agents dragging the Bishop out of his Sacramento compound were on every site, but vids of Linus being carried from his exclusive honeymoon suite on a stretcher amid a sea of police were trending.

Baniker watched the spectacle unfold from his favorite stool at O'Malley's. He was on his second double when she came in. His eyes didn't move from the monitors. "Let me guess," he said. "He hurt himself trying to sneak out a ventilation duct?"

"Something like that." Lucy ordered a vodka neat and sat down beside him. "How'd you know? Most of the sites are guessing attempted suicide. Honestly, if you'd asked me beforehand, I would have bet on him blowing his brains out."

"No, he's too limp for that."

"You're taking this better than I expected," Lucy said.

Baniker looked at Lucy for the first time since she'd come in. She'd traded in the stylish dress for a simple gray suit, and her hair was up in a tight bun. Only her effervescent blue eyes still reminded him of her mother.

"You thought I'd be shocked that you used me to expose your new family's dirty laundry?"

"Hurt, maybe." Lucy said. "Angry."

"Well, maybe I was a little of both. I knew someone was trying to play me, I just didn't think it was you." Baniker downed the last of his drink and signaled the bartender for another round. He still wasn't sure why he hadn't suspected Lucy was the one trying to manipulate him. "Once I realized what the evidence was, it all fell into place. Then I only had one choice, really, no matter how I felt about it."

"You could have given me the evidence. You said we were covered by client privilege."

"There are some good lawyers who'd debate that. But you would have just had to find someone else to turn it over."

"True," Lucy said.

"The government will seize all the church's assets."

"Which government?"

Baniker shrugged. "I don't know. Maybe all of them."

"It'll take them a while to sort things out. Most of the money will still be there when they do."

Baniker figured Lucy would have a few dozen numbered accounts at Lignore's before then. "You thought it all out pretty good, didn't you?"

The bartender put their drinks in front of them. Baniker held up his glass. "I never got to toast the bride."

Lucy touched her drink to his.

"Still," Baniker said, "I get that you knew about

the church's involvement in the drug running—but how'd you know about Carr? He was a nobody."

"I told you, I overheard Linus and the Bishop talking."

"I dug into the church's accounts before I went to Venus. There's no evidence of a two-million credit payout. Not in the time frame you mentioned."

"Maybe I misheard them."

"There is a record of payments from your personal account, though."

Lucy shrugged, but her nonchalance was forced.

"You intercepted Carr—paid him off—your husband and father-in-law never knew it was coming."

"When Carr realized he'd been running Damage for the church, he tried to contact Linus. They had known each other like I said, but Linus used to run errands for Carr, not the other way around—my husband isn't the brightest star in the constellation. I took the call, and Carr let on enough for me to see what was going on."

"You must have been stunned. Tell me, were you engaged before or after you learned all this?"

Lucy did an unconvincing impression of being hurt. "I suppose I deserved that."

"So you paid off Carr, and then came here and put me on the case just in time to catch him *after* you were conveniently married. This will destroy the entire Prosperity church. You may be the most successful gold digger in history."

Lucy reddened. "That's not a crime, is it?"

"No," Baniker admitted.

"I know you don't like me very much, Mr. Baniker. I can't say I blame you after what I did, but—for what it's worth—I regret having to involve you. I needed your help. That's all there was to it. I deposited a large payment for your services in your account. I hope it will go some way toward salving your wounds."

With that, Lucy downed her drink and put the empty glass back on the bar. She got up to leave, but Baniker put his hand on her arm.

"Just one question..."

"You want to know if my mother knew?"

"Did she?"

"I told you she said you would help me."

Baniker watched Lucy go—her walk so much like her mother's it tore at his heart. At least it would have if he were the sentimental type.

Which he wasn't.

A fugitive hides from his pursuers, as below him, parents tend a sick child. But this is a very special kind of fugitive, because he is haunted by . . .

VOICES

By Alan Amrhine

I hid there in the attic of the old house, quiet and still amid the cobwebs and dust. If a board creaked, it was the weight of old timbers, not any nervous movement on my part. If the air whistled, it was wind through the eaves, not my anxious breathing. Nothing was disturbed. I had pulled my *essence* back into myself—I could feel the energy tingle beneath my skin, but I held it tight. I had made myself as bland and gray as the surroundings. A brown recluse spider, tickling its way across a web just inches from my face, paused as if sensing my presence, then moved again along its thready path. *See! I am no threat, no menace, not even to the smallest creature. Why then do they pursue me?*

How long had they hunted me? A laugh welled in my chest, almost escaped my lips. There was something funny in the fact I did not know how long they had hounded me. What I did know was that they were relentless, and that time was of no matter to them. *Why can't they leave me in peace? They should stay where they belong.* I leaned back slowly, ever so slowly, so as not to disturb the dust that floated in slices of sunlight, and closed my eyes. I was light as a puff of air, inconsequential as a raindrop in a torrential storm. They would not find me. I would be safe here for a while. If only I could quiet the voices in my head.

I knew my pursuers could not hear the voices. The murmurings, even the shouts, were no threat to reveal my presence. The voices were mine to hear, and mine alone. I had treasured them in the beginning, and enjoyed pleasing them. How many times had I killed at their urging, just to make them happy? But, for too long now, they yammered and mewled incessantly—more voices each day—leap-frogging one another, scratching and clawing over one another, in their insistence for my attention.

My eyes snapped open. The light was decomposing into darkness—a blood-red beam trickled through a hole in the attic wall—but I could still see well enough. My senses were quite exquisite. The hairs on my arms rustled silently, like millipede legs, conveying the coolness of the coming night air. I did not like the dark—in fact, there was something loathsome about the dark. But I did not fear it. I did not fear anything, except *them*.

"How is she this evening?" The voice scraped against my eardrums, loud, *audible*, differing from the rest of the voices that rumbled in my head. It came from below, from the room beneath the attic— a man's raspy voice.

"I don't notice any difference," said a woman, her voice tight with emotion. "Doc Goodman brought some quinine by today. He said it might help bring down her fever. She's still so awfully hot."

I leaned, ever so gently, ever so slowly, toward a crack of yellow light poking up through the corner of the floor. I positioned my eyes close to the tiny fissure and looked down. An oil lamp danced light about the room below, splashing the color of sunshine against the walls and then—as it flickered, in the instant it receded, for a bare moment—lining the creases and shadows with the color of dried blood. A young girl, damp and flushed, lay abed in the middle of the room. A woman perched on a wooden chair at the bedside, wringing a cloth in a basin of water. She placed it on the little girl's forehead and started to sob. The man, standing just inside the doorway, moved closer. He placed his left hand on the woman's shoulder, crumpled his hat brim with his right. His strong shoulders sagged under the weight of what could have been mountains.

"That's our Amy there, John—" The woman collapsed against the bed, resting her cheek on the girl's hand.

The man dropped his hat, held the woman by both shoulders. He looked up at the ceiling. "God," he said, and his voice caught in his throat. "I don't have the words of a preacher. All I have is what's in my heart . . . our hearts." He squeezed his wife tighter. "Please help our daughter. She is only seven. Amy was so happy about starting school next week now that the town has a teacher. Please help her—" The man's face contorted and he looked down quickly. Two large teardrops hit the floor simultaneously, mixed with the dust, sank into the rough planks.

Drama—excellent, excellent drama! I laughed, softly. *Pain, faith, need, hope—it's all there.* Oh, how I loved it. My chest swelled with pride for the family below. This is how it was meant to be—what an excellent, excellent example of the human condition.

I would have killed the girl later, of course, to reward the couple by shortening their angst, but, *NO!* I could not afford to be careless. Some of my essence might already have flared with my laugh, and I could ill afford that. I leaned away from the crack in the floor, willed myself to become bland, washed out against my surroundings. In my stillness, the other voices pounded in my head. *The voices!* So loud, but I knew my pursuers could not hear them—though they thumped against my temples, ground down into my teeth. I hoped my momentary lapse in control was not enough that my pursuers had detected me. With luck, I would be—

All around me, the air burned with every color of the spectrum. They materialized, one by one, and stood as a group in the center of the attic, beneath the rough-hewn beams of the roof. They stood with right arms extended, with auras blazing, and I found that I could not move. They were mostly younger than I, strong in their vigor, and there were six of them. I was held fast by their power, manacled with a force that even I could not overcome.

"It is over, old friend," said the leader of the group, more ancient than the rest, his voice soft and rolling like the thunder that chased heat lightning on a summer evening. "It is time to come home and rest."

"This is my creation, Nah-Vel. It is against code for you to be in my universe uninvited."

"Normally, yes, you would be right. But, as you know, you have incurred special circumstances that necessitated our coming."

"Special circumstances." I spat the words. "All the Architects are jealous of me. Where have you seen such light? In what other universe? A billion billion stars flame with controlled abandon, piercing the darkness, burning virtually forever. Which of your cold and dim creations can compare?" I glared at the young Architects. Most of them looked away.

Nah-Vel nodded slowly, then raised his eyes to look at me. "Be that as it may, you have transgressed. You have become . . . damaged."

"Damaged?" I sneered at my old friend. "How do you imagine I'm damaged?"

He sighed. "For one, you have speckled your worlds with living, sentient creatures, creatures that have finely tuned nervous systems. And then you set a system in place where these creatures are consumed alive by one another, experiencing incredible pain and fear that cannot be turned off, even when their ending is imminent."

Gasps arose from the young members of the group.

"But the system works," I said. "Don't you see? That is the genius of it. My world's life systems stay in balance, and the species learn and grow and survive. Without pain and fear, the system would not work."

In that instant I brought all my power to bear to break free of this bondage. I focused all the energy that exploded a universe into existence many eons ago, but the effect was nil. I was able to muster little more than a shoulder shrug against the combined power of six Architects.

"It is no use, my friend," the ancient Architect said. "It is done."

"But we are among the first, among the oldest, of our race. Our creations were in full bloom before any of these Architects were even begotten."

He nodded, his eyes tinged with sadness.

"And I am the best!"

"Yes," said Nah-Vel. "You were the best of all the Architects. But, in your illness, you tried to make yourself . . . something more."

I laughed, some unknown giddiness overtaking me. "Look—look downstairs in this very dwelling, old friend. The high creatures of this particular world—I created them in our image! They are magnificent!"

"You know that is also against code—"

"Nevertheless, they are fantastic creations. I made them in our image—but I made them to hurt, I made them to bleed, I made them . . . to need and worship *me*, their Creator."

Another gasp arose from the group of younger Architects.

Nah-Vel shook his head. "That is an abuse of the highest order."

"I am God. In this universe, *I am GOD!*" I laughed—at nothing, at everything.

"We're going home now, Yah-Weh."

"I can hear them. I hear every one of them. They talk to me, they *pray* to me," I said, boasting. Then my voice cracked. "The voices—so many voices. I can't make them stop. Help me, old friend. They never stop . . . so very many voices . . ."

Ain't it the truth? Work in a bar long enough and you'll meet everybody.

SOMEBODY'S GOTTA DO IT

By Mark Lee Taylor

So this guy walks into a bar, right?

Sorry about that. Oldest line in the book.

But really, that's how it starts. This guy walks into Rick's Corner Bar, and pauses just inside. He's backlit by the afternoon sun coming through the door, just a silhouette, but already I can tell he's got problems.

I've been tending bar for a long time, and I can tell at a glance when a fella's got something to unload, or forget about, or drown. Sometimes it's the posture. Downcast eyes. Sloppy dress or a three-day beard. The set of the shoulders, the way they walk. Nervous twitches.

Sometimes it's some subliminal tip-off that even I don't understand. I just know.

Yeah, I used that word. I might be just a bartender and an electrician, but that doesn't mean I don't read, okay?

Anyway, this guy's one of the subliminal ones. I can't tell you how I know he's got issues, I just know that I know.

Nothing unusual about the way he stopped just inside the door. A lot of people do that, to get their bearings and pick out a seat. In daylight, almost everyone does, to let their eyes adjust to the darkness in here.

Not that Rick's Corner Bar is a cave or anything.

We have two windows, one on the south wall and one on the east. Depending on the time of year, we might draw the curtains on them, or we might not, but either way at least a little light dribbles in. We even have light fixtures in the ceiling that we turn on sometimes. We are a thoroughly modern establishment. But it's dark in here compared to outside on a sunny afternoon like this one. The walls are painted a dark shade of grayish-tan, something my wife calls "taupe." She refuses to talk about normal colors like gray, tan, red, green. Everything is taupe or chartreuse or magenta or teal. What are you gonna do? You marry an artist, it comes with the territory.

Anyway, the floor, the bar, and the furniture are all wood, stained a color just a bit lighter than chocolate. Rick Tolliver, the current owner, had it redone a couple of years ago when he bought it. He said the dark colors and the wood give it an air of refinement. And I think he's right.

Anyway, the guy makes his decision, I guess, and starts moving through the room toward the bar. Now I can see him better. Tall guy, fortyish, I'm guessing a lawyer or a banker, from the way he's dressed. We used to get mostly blue-collar types in here, but after the renovation, a few suits started showing up. We get all types now.

This guy isn't one of our regulars, though. I got a good memory for faces, and this is the first time I've laid eyes on his.

This early in the afternoon, the bar's not very crowded. Three tinbangers sitting at the bar talking shop, a twenty-something couple sitting at a window table, wrapped up in their own little world. Plenty of empty seats to choose from.

The new guy grabs a stool at the bar and plops down into it, rests his arms on the edge. Brown eyes, great hair, face like a movie star. At this point I'm thinkin', *Can't be woman problems.*

Top three things guys complain about in a bar: women, jobs, and money. All three are closely interrelated, of course. This guy's problem must be his job or his finances, or both.

"How's it going?" I say to him.

"Not so bad. Can I get a Jack and Coke?"

"Sure thing." Gotta admit, I'm a little surprised. I almost had the idea he was going to order some kind of foo-foo drink, like a pina colada or a daiquiri. I like him already. So I make him the drink and I make sure he sees me put a little extra Jack in there, and I put it in front of him. "Don't tell anybody," I say. "You look like you could use it."

"Pffft," the guy says. "You have no idea."

I laugh. "Betcha I do. I've heard it all in here."

He takes a pull off his drink and says, "What's your name?"

"Matt."

He sighs, and says, "Let me ask you something, Matt."

During the pause, I notice that he hasn't offered his own name, or his hand. A little odd, but guys with problems aren't always quite themselves, so I don't take offense.

"How old are you?" he says.

"Forty-two," I say, a bit taken aback. "Just last week."

"Happy belated," he says.

"Thanks."

"Married?"

"Yup."

"Kids?"

"Two. Nineteen and sixteen. Both boys."

He frowns and says, "You supporting two teenagers as a bartender?"

"Hell, no. This is my second job. I work nights as an electrician. Matter of fact, I'm getting ready to clock out of here in about an hour, and go to my 'day job.' " I always get a kick out of dropping that line. My main job, my 'day job,' is a night job, and my second job is tending bar, in the daytime. Some people get it, and some don't. I glance at him to see if he's one of the ones that gets it.

Nope.

"Electrician, huh? Pay well?"

Now this is getting a little personal, but again, I cut the guy some slack, 'cause I got a feeling this is his way of getting around to what he really wants to talk about. "It's okay, I guess. I do a few side jobs. Put all these lights in here for the new owner. But it's still not enough to put a kid through college, not by itself. You do what you gotta do, right? Hell, I'd take a third job if I could fit it in."

He sighs again. "How's things with the wife? Hunky dory?"

I frown. Things are just fine with me and my wife, who happens to be an angel in disguise, and normally I don't mind talking about that, but I think the flow of information should start running the other direction pretty soon.

"Well, I don't see her as much as I'd like, but yeah, we're fine," I say. "I take it yours ain't happy with you?"

He looks surprised, then says, "No, no, that's not it. I'm not married."

"Girlfriend, then?"

"No. No. You don't get it. It's, um… It's my job."

Then why all the questions about my family? I'm thinking. "Oh," I say. "What line are you in?"

He looks at me for a good five seconds before he says, "I have the world's dirtiest job."

At this I just have to laugh. "I never would've

guessed that, the way you're dressed."

"It's true," he says, and takes another drink. "You ever seen that Mike Rowe show, *Dirty Jobs*?"

"Yeah," I say. "Makes me feel better about mine."

"Mine is dirtier than any you've ever seen on that show."

I look at his nails. Not a trace of black under 'em. Look like they might've been manicured, for Christ's sake. How dirty could his job be? "Okay" I say. "What is it, then?"

He doesn't answer, but turns away from me and stares out the window. I let him have his moment to get hold of himself, and when he finally turns back, I could swear I see tears in his eyes.

"I really hate this," he says.

"Friend," I say, "You don't have to talk about it if you don't want to. But I can see you're really sufferin'. Don't know if I've ever seen anybody get so worked up over a job. Is it that important? Maybe it's time to move on."

"Can't do that. I wish I could. Really, I do."

"Why not?"

"It's that important. It has to be done. It's cliché as hell, but somebody's gotta do it. And I'm elected, I'm the lucky guy. I wish I could get out of it, but if I quit... You just can't imagine the chaos." He pauses. "Hell, I better just shut up."

I nod my head. "Government?"

He takes a drink, looks up at me. "Sort of."

"I understand. There's different kinds of dirt. Workin' for just about any of those outfits with a three-letter acronym can be pretty dirty, I guess."

"The dirtiest."

"Sorry to hear that, fella."

He takes another sip from his drink, then puts it, half-empty, back on the bar. "I shouldn't be putting this on you, Matt. But it's so hard, this job.

It's killing me. And I can't talk to anybody else about it. You're the one guy that it's okay for me to talk to."

"Me? Why?"

"Because ... listen, I'm sorry. This is so wrong of me. Just because it's okay for me to talk to you doesn't make it right."

"I don't mind, really. Believe me, I get this all the time. Sometimes I can even help people, and then I can go home, you know, feeling a little better about myself, too."

"I have to go," he says, and gets up from his stool. He throws a few bills on the bar. "Been nice talking to you."

"Same. Take care."

"And I'm sorry."

"Not a problem."

He holds his hand out for me to shake, and I take it. He's got a nice firm grip. Then he turns and walks out the door without another word. For a split second, I see his silhouette as he passes through the doorway, and I swear it didn't look like the silhouette of a guy in a business suit. It looked like...

Ah, never mind. My eyes must be playin' tricks on me.

Whew. Weird dude. Like I said, we get all types in here.

I pick up his glass, pour what's left of his drink into the drain, and drop the glass into soapy water. I scoop his money off the bar and run the rag over the condensation ring his glass left.

On my way to the register, I feel a sharp pain in my chest, and it makes me make a sound, something like "Gurkk!"

I freeze in place. Oh, man, this hurts. In a few seconds, the pain goes shooting down my left arm. I break out in a sweat, and all of a sudden I feel like I need to throw up. I can't breathe. Oh, shit, this ain't good. This ain't good at all.

I've heard that your life flashes before your eyes, but that ain't true, not true at all, at least not for me. What flashes before my eyes is all the stuff I didn't do. Things I left hanging, loose ends my wife'll have to tie up, places I never got to see, family events I missed 'cause I was working, times I didn't tell my wife and kids I loved 'em when I should have, important things I never got to tell my boys, *things they need to know to survive in this world, dammit!*

Panic sets in. I can't go now. There's so much left to do. Besides, I'm too young. It's not fair!

I drop the money. It feels like somebody's sitting on my chest. Oh, God, it hurts so bad. I go down to my knees, thinking about my wife and my boys, wondering if they'll be okay.

I don't remember it happening, but somehow I'm face down on the floor now. I see people's feet coming toward me, and I hear voices, but they sound like they're underwater. It's hard to understand 'em, and even harder to care. It would be so easy to just ... slip away.

As my vision starts to go black, I realize it doesn't hurt anymore. The panic is gone, and a calm settles over me like a warm blanket on a cold January night. I feel ... peaceful. It's okay. I accept it.

The last thing I think about is the look in that guy's eyes as he shook my hand, and I feel his pain. He was right. There's no dirtier job than his.

Here's an interesting story from Amy Bock that reminds us why we prefer to drive cars.

AND TO THINK WE USED TO HOP ON TRAINS

By Amy Bock

As Greg made his way to the ticket counter, a woman smiled at him. For a minute he thought of stopping; but he had more important things to deal with.

"How can the train be late?" Greg demanded as he got to the counter.

The ticket handler, who had a small face and large glasses, blinked. "Excuse me?"

"I need to be in Albany tonight. At this rate, I'll be there at ten, and by the time I've checked in, found my room, and unpacked, it will be *midnight*. I have a job interview, you know!"

"There's nothing I can do. I'm sorry."

"No, you're not. See, you get to go home. Do you have a husband?"

"I have a dog . . ."

"I don't even get to go home to my dog! I have to go to a hotel room!"

"It's a job interview, right?"

Greg turned. The woman who'd smiled before had spoken, and this time, he got a proper look at her.

Her pixie-cut hair was brown with a few purple highlights. Her eyes were blue . . . very blue. She had an upturned nose and was wearing mermaid earrings.

51

"Yeah," Greg said. "Why?"

"If you get the job, you're going to live there anyway. So in a way, you are going home."

"I wasn't talking to you," Greg snapped.

"When you talk loud enough for everyone to hear, you're talking to everyone. I was *trying* to mind my own business"—the woman pointed to the book in her hand—"but it's hard to read when there's some guy losing his shit in front of you."

"I'M NOT LOSING MY SHIT!" Greg yelled.

The woman raised her eyebrows. Greg turned back to the ticket handler, but she was now talking to someone else.

Greg realized that the only empty seat was right next to Miss Nosy. Greg grudgingly sat down and took his coat off.

"That's better," she said. "If it makes you feel better, I'm waiting too. Not to go anywhere, but . . ."

Greg pulled out his phone and checked for messages.

"Oh," the woman said, sounding irritated, "it's like that."

That got Greg's attention. "Like what?"

"Nothing." The woman's eyes rolled up to the light on the ceiling, then down to the book she'd picked up again.

"No." Greg lowered the book from her face. "Like what?" He knew he'd been insulted, but didn't quite know *how*.

"I make polite conversation in an attempt to cheer you up, and you look at your phone. Is there really anything on your phone that you didn't just see five minutes ago?"

"Emails. Voicemails. Text messages."

"That's why I tossed my cell phone in a lake," she said. "My boyfriend was pissed."

"I guess that's who you're waiting for?"

"Yeah." She toyed with one of her earrings.

"Is he coming from Albany?"

"No. Boston. He's in a band and they were playing there . . . I had to work. Or at least," she added with a giggle, "that's what I told him."

Greg raised his eyebrows. "What's the real reason?"

"By the way," the woman interrupted, "I just realized I didn't even get your name."

"Oh. Greg."

The woman smiled; she had a pretty smile. "I'm Emily."

"Emily," Greg repeated slowly. At first glance, such a plain name on a very not plain woman was almost jarring; but it fit, somehow. Gave her a bit of softness behind her blunt demeanor, just like her eyes . . .

"Greg," Emily returned with a laugh. "So have you been to Albany before?"

"No," Greg admitted. "I just needed a change of atmosphere."

"What was her name?" Emily asked. More softness.

"Whose name?"

Emily gave him a look. "It was a girl, right?"

Instantly Greg thought of her red hair . . . the way her laugh carried through the walls . . ."Jenna," Greg replied. "We broke up. Also, I hate the job I have now. Albany wasn't the first place I thought of when I considered second chances, but it's somewhere, right?"

"Albany's okay," Emily said. "I was born there, actually. All my family's there. I've been dying to visit, but we don't have the money. My parents visit often enough, but it's been ages since I've seen my sister."

Emily said the last part with sadness in her

voice.

"How could your boyfriend afford to go to Boston?"

"He was going for work," Emily said.

"His band, you mean?"

"It's an investment," Emily said as though this should be obvious. But she wasn't looking at him.

Before Greg could stop himself, he asked her, "How can a girl as honest as you be so dishonest with yourself?"

Emily's eyes narrowed. "Excuse me?"

"You want to go home, but you're not going home so a guy who couldn't even be bothered to make the train on time can play in a band you don't even like."

Emily was glaring now. "Stop. It."

"Do you even like the guy? You haven't said his name once."

"How dare you!" Emily exclaimed. "Do you know what he's done for me?"

"What has he done for you?"

"He's . . ." Emily stopped. "Well, you're one to talk. What did you do to your girlfriend that she dumped you?"

"She cheated on me with her boss."

"Exact—oh."

There was an uncomfortable silence; for several minutes they avoided looking at each other.

"It's hard," Emily said quietly. "My sister, she can't make the trip because she's in a wheelchair."

"I'm sorry."

"Yeah." Emily was tying her shoes now. "Maybe that's why I left Albany. The guilt. I was driving that night."

Emily leaned back into her chair. "And now I can't even be there for her."

"Maybe you can be," Greg said suddenly.

"How?" Emily asked. "I already told you, our travel money's been spent."

"Come to Albany with me, then," Greg told her. "I'll get you a ticket."

Emily snorted in disbelief. "You'll get me a ticket when we've only just met?"

"It's the least I can do for disturbing you while you were trying to read."

"But what about my boyfriend? And—I don't even have anything packed!"

"I think I know you pretty well," Greg began, "and you seem like the sort of girl who'll figure that part out."

Emily's lips twitched, and Greg thought she was holding back a grin. "Okay. But I doubt there'll be any tickets left."

Greg went back up to the counter. The bespectacled lady said, without batting an eye, "I told you, the train has been delayed."

"No, it's not that. I want an extra ticket."

"An extra ticket?"

"Yes."

The woman shook her head. "Good thing for you the train was late."

As soon as Greg returned to Emily, she stood up excitedly.

"Thank you!" she gasped. "You didn't have to do that!"

"Yes, I did."

"I have to call my sister." Emily pulled a phone out of her pocket.

"Wait a minute," Greg said. "I thought you didn't have a phone?"

"Oh—I got a new one."

She held the phone to her ear, and after a minute said, "Tara? It's me. I have news. . ." Emily eyed Greg and he got the impression that this was a private conversation. So he gestured for her to watch his things while he made for the men's room.

When he returned, she was gone, as were both of their things.

"Emily?" Greg called loudly.

Suddenly, announcements overhead called all passengers to Greg's train.

But where was Emily?

Finally, Greg caught sight of her with another man. He tried to get to her, but the crowd kept pushing him away.

"Emily!" Greg yelled as they reached the train, finally catching up to her. The other man was nowhere to be seen now; maybe he'd gotten ahead of her.

Emily didn't seem to hear him. She handed the conductor her ticket and got on.

"Here's mine," Greg said, practically panting now.

But it wasn't in his pocket . . .

"Sir? Do you have your ticket?"

"I—that woman had it!" Greg said. "She'll tell you!"

"Miss!" The conductor called to Emily, heading her way. Greg waited patiently; after a minute, the conductor came back.

"She says she's not with you," he said. "Better luck next time, son."

By the time Greg managed to get back to the counter, then back to the train with the taker, the train was long gone.

* * *

"So how'd you pull this one off?" Doug asked.

"Just a minute, let me take these awful earrings off," Melanie said. "I can't believe someone paid for these."

She threw the small mermaids out the window. "That's better. Anyway, I decided to put my drama classes to use. I found some nice guy, got him to tell me all of his boring problems, then I made up some sob story about my sister being in a wheelchair. Next thing I know, two free tickets."

"And to think we used to hop on trains. So . . . how do we pull it off next time?"

"Well," Melanie began, "the wheelchair story worked *really* well for me . . ."

Mysterious goings on in the valley, but only one man is bold enough to challenge . . .

THE SIREN

By Joe Long

The siren. The siren coming from that damnable mountain. High noon, just like every day. It rose with an unrelenting urgency and hung heavy in the air. It covered the valley like a rolling storm and stretched out through the sky to touch the clouds. It rang for several minutes and then died. It left behind a silence so resonant, it was deafening compared to the siren itself.

The people of the valley paused, lowering their heads in something that wasn't quite fear, nor reverence, but was something close and otherwise indescribable. They stood still in fields, or in their kitchens, or eased their horses to a stop, and waited for it to pass.

Today, Weston Holt did not lower his head. He raised his eyes to the mountain and cursed.

He couldn't say exactly what made him look. Nobody ever looked at the mountain, an imposing peak that split the pale sky in two. It loomed over the valley, casting its shadow on the fields and farms just as much as on the hearts of the people below. It was a thing no one spoke of. A thing they pushed into the backs of their minds. A ghost that haunted them.

Weston Holt finished filling his water skin at the old rusty pump and climbed atop his mare. He kicked his heels into her sides and galloped off toward town. A cloud of brown dust shot up and hung in the air as the horse's hoofs dug into the dry dirt floor covering the valley. The landscape was dotted with a handful of sickly trees, firs and other evergreens, though they had scarcely ever actually been green. Scattered amongst the trees were rusted metal shells of devices long forgotten, hulking machines with gears and dials and engines. Things that had no place in this world anymore.

He rode with purpose. In his head, he felt a tugging, as if a thought, long burrowed, was trying to chew its way out. His mind began to itch. He pressed in and rode harder.

Weston made his way into town and to the saloon and hitched his mare to a post. With palms against his temples, he pushed through the bat-wing doors and stumbled inside. A cold sunlight pushed through cracks in the aging walls, casting an uneven, jagged light into the gloom. It was a good-sized room, with a bar lining the back and several small, round tables along the sides. A handful of people sat at the bar, some already in their cups despite the early hour, with others just milling about because they had nowhere better to be. Behind the bar, Bennett wiped dirt off a glass with an even dirtier rag. Weston rushed across the room and put his hand on the shoulder of a man who was slumped over the bar like a sack of potatoes gone to rot.

"Gideon!" called Weston, with a shout pushed through a groan. "Gideon, you've got to help me!"

The man called Gideon turned slowly, his eyelids heavy like fog. He took a labored drink from his cup and sat it back down sharply. His wide face worked hard as he steadied his thoughts.

"What?"

"You've got to help," Weston replied impatiently. His mind itched again, harder than before. He clamped his eyes shut and grabbed his head. "We've got to go. To the—to the—" He sputtered, trying to get the words out, but they were fading. His head pulsed, and the words were gone. "I don't remember," he said, in a voice so sad it was startling. "I can't." He sat down and lowered his head to the bar.

"It's all right," said Gideon in a voice that was sympathetic but gruff. "Bennett, a drink for my friend, please."

Bennett complied with a grimy, lukewarm mug. Weston took it nonetheless, and gladly.

"You've had it rough—yes, you have, Westy," said Gideon. "Been to hell and back, more than the rest of us. Mayhap you need a good rest, is all." Gideon trailed off at this and disappeared back into his drink.

Rest. Rest was one thing Weston couldn't do. When he rested he saw her face. Her haunting face. His wife, taken by the pox. He had begged death to take him in her stead, but he was left here, alone in this godforsaken valley, a dirty, dry hell in its own right. No. No rest.

What had he just been doing?

The pounding in his head increased. He could hear his thoughts echo and grow louder until they were a piercing din.

He flung the mug off the bar with his hand. It went flying and shattered against the floor. The crash filled the saloon like a warning.

Like an alarm.

Like a goddamned siren.

"Blazes, West, you're gonna pay for that!" growled Bennett. "What in the hell has gotten into you?"

"The mountain!" Weston spat.

"What?" gaped Gideon, eyes narrowed.

"To the mountain. That's where I'm going. Come with me! Help me!"

The quiet room suddenly grew quieter still, as if the very air around them was holding its breath. All eyes looked to Weston and then quickly looked away. Gideon, however, had already drunk himself some courage.

"Quiet!" Gideon hissed with a venom that seemed to surprise even himself. He continued in a hoarse whisper. "Have you gone mad? What are you even talking about? You know the mountain's off limits!" He shooed Weston away angrily with a callused hand.

Weston could not back down now. The pulsing in his head was fueling him now, though whether it was to action or just rage was still to be seen. "I'm talking about that goddamned mountain," he replied, pointing in the direction of the great hulking form, his voice rising from a growl to a roar. "I'm talking about the siren. It mocks us!" He pounded his fist on the bar, glasses jumping in his wake. He couldn't recall making a fist, but there it was, his fingernails digging deep into his palm.

Bennett barked at him. "You will calm down this instant, West, or I will have you out of here!" The sheer force of his voice hung in the air between them, startling Weston. His head stopped throbbing, and his rage subsided. For just a moment, he felt clear. He felt present.

"I'm-I'm sorry. And I'm sorry about the glass, Benny. I am. But come on. Don't you want to know? Know what it is? Why no one talks about it?"

"We're just not supposed to," said Gideon in a gruff hush. "We're just not. And you better not let the Constable hear you going on about it." Gideon wearily shook his head.

"Blasted Constable," Weston growled.

"You called?" came a thick, dour voice from the saloon's entrance. Like molasses on jagged rocks.

Bennett blustered. "C-C-Constable. G-Good day to you, sir."

"Save it, Benn," the Constable said with a grimace. He walked into the saloon, slowly, his boots and spurs making a loud click-whir, click-whir with each step. Sunlight caught his silver badge, making it shine bright against his black vest. He stopped halfway into the saloon and gave his black Stetson a tug. He twitched his gray handlebar moustache and let out a dramatic sigh.

Gideon spun around, sobered. His face was a moon. Weston got to his feet, his body plotting escape.

"Hear you're up to no good, there, West." The Constable never seemed to call anyone by their full name, as if it wasn't worth his time. "Hear you're making trouble."

Weston eyed the Constable carefully, as well as the two deputies who had followed him in, careful of what he said next.

The Constable grew tired of the silence. "Why don't you just head on home, boy, and sleep this whole thing off? Can ya do that for me?" Arrogance seeped through the Constable's voice like a river overflowing.

Weston moved his mouth, but he found no words to fill it with.

One of the deputies stepped forward quickly and poked Weston in the chest. He had a weaselly face and slicked-back hair. His voice was high and nasal. "Mebbe you didn't hear what the good Constable said to you."

Weston glared at him. His jaw clenched, and his hands curled into fists again.

"Now, deputy, give the man some room," said the

Constable, his face like a wolf upon sheep.

"Yeah, don't scare 'im now," said the other deputy, licking his lips and stroking his goatee. He began to laugh, a laugh so bereft of humor that the only thing left in it was cruelty.

Weston felt them pressing in. The laugh. The finger in his chest. The Constable's horrible grin, pulled back to reveal menacing teeth.

The siren rang in his head.

And from somewhere deep within him, somewhere he didn't recognize, a voice rose. Deep and angry and with a conviction he had never known before. "You get the hell out of my way. I'm going to that goddamned mountain."

"You know very well, boy," the Constable said, his words a very tribute to disdain, "that the mountain is off limits." His mouth went from grin to sneer.

Everything that followed happened in an instant.

The first deputy grabbed Weston by the shoulders. Weston took the deputy's wrist and twisted it hard, forcing him to the ground. The wrist made a sharp, snapping sound. The second deputy choked on his laugh and ran toward them. Weston greeted him with a firm punch to his jaw, and a second to his gut. The deputy howled and doubled over. Weston began kicking the first one, who was on his knees, gripping his wrist and crying for help.

Weston was not a violent man, but today was different.

The Constable reached for his revolver. With what looked like one giant step, he bounded across the saloon and placed it against Weston's temple.

The click of the gun's hammer cocked back loudly, full of malice.

Weston stopped, and his body seemed to sag.

"Now you done made a mess of things," said the

Constable quietly, the words seething through his mouth. "I am a patient man and I gave you a fair chance, but assaulting an officer of the law is unforgivable, yes it is. In the lockup with you today, and the rope tomorrow." The Constable's words were grim, but his eyes were alive.

"No!" Gideon protested, but his fire had run out, and he shrank with a single glance from the Constable.

"You," the Constable called to the goateed deputy. "Put the cuffs on him and help me get him to the station. You," he motioned to the weasel on the floor, "get off your sissy ass and get yourself to the doc, pronto."

The deputy walked over to Weston and gave him a swift jab in the stomach before putting the cuffs on him. He grabbed Weston's arm tightly and walked him out of the saloon. Weston shuffled out, his head hung limp.

The Constable looked around the saloon and tugged at his hat before leaving. "You all have a pleasant day, now."

* * *

Weston Holt now lay on a cot in the holding cell of the Constable's station. The deputies had finally given up teasing him through the bars, and had gone back into town in search of more trouble. Weston closed his eyes as his head resumed its thrum. He pushed his palms against his eye sockets and groaned, but it did no good. He opened them again and saw the mountain through the bars of his window. It was staring right at him, boring into him. He curled into a ball and slipped into a fevered dream.

And she was there.

Annabeth.

Every night that he dreamed of her, her face was less and less until it was finally just a blur, out of focus and out of reach. He could still smell her scent, lavender and wildflowers. His fingertips could still remember the touch of her skin. It was comforting, yet made the loss more profound. She stood before him, her blue dress rippling in some unseen wind, her long hair hanging in tight, dark curls. His body felt flush in her presence. She reached out to him, as she did every night. But this time, she spoke.

"Weston!" she called, her voice an echo of itself. "Weston! You're falling so far away from me!" The dread in her voice pierced West's heart. Tears stung his eyes and he reached out, her name on his lips. She buckled, as if being pulled back and shrieked. "Find me!"

And then she was gone.

* * *

He awoke with a bucket of cold water dumped on his head. The deputies stood above him, leering and laughing.

"Almost time to be strung up," said the weasel-faced deputy, his wrist now in a splint. "Best start saying yer prayers now."

"Give him some room," said the Constable, leaning against the cell's doorway with his hand resting on his revolver.

The deputies backed up, and Weston slowly got to his feet, wiping the wet hair out of his face.

"I'm not an unkind man, Weston," the Constable said, "so I have provided you with a last meal." He motioned to a table set up just outside the cell, with one chair and a plate of food, gray and cold.

Weston shuffled out and sat down. The deputies took up spots by the station's door. The Constable sat with his feet propped up on his desk. Despite himself, Weston dug in.

"Easy now, don't choke. The town would hate to lose a show." The Constable watched him like a circling vulture. "What's got you all rattled anyhow, boy, that'd make you want to break the laws of this good town and assault these fine men?"

"The mountain," Weston growled through a full mouth.

"You know very well the mountain is off limits," replied the Constable.

"Why?" replied Weston.

"It just is. It's dangerous. And it's the law," the Constable said, matter of factly.

"Whose law? And why? *Why* is it dangerous?" Weston swallowed down rage, careful not to make his situation worse.

The Constable looked at him like he didn't understand the question.

Weston felt flushed. His mind started itching. It wouldn't be long before it was pounding again. "Look, there's something dangerous about that mountain, but it has nothing to do with us going up there. It's a danger to us now. Right now. It's ... doing something to us. I can't explain it, but I can feel it. I know. What's the siren? Can you at least tell me that?"

The Constable shrugged. "Means high noon."

"No," Weston said forcefully. "It's not some damned cuckoo clock coming out of that thing. It's unnatural. It shouldn't be. You know it as well as I do." His jaws were clenched and his eyes drilled into the Constable's.

"You can take your paranoia to the grave, friend. Law is law. Everyone else is smart enough to know that. Meal's over." With a septic grin, the Constable gave the table a sharp kick. The plate shattered, uneaten food spilling across the floor. He motioned to his deputies, who grabbed Weston by the arms and forced him outside.

A small crowd of townspeople had already begun to gather around the gallows in the town square. It was seldom used but that made it no less threatening. A noose hung limply. Weston was pushed up the steps to the top of the platform. The sun beat down hard, and Weston felt the weight of it on him. He saw Gideon in the crowd, and Bennett, too. They held their hats to their chests and looked away.

His hands were bound. He stepped up on the box, and a deputy looped the noose around his neck. The preacher had joined them on the stand and was giving last rites. Weston's head starting buzzing. The sun was right in his eyes. That meant it was almost high noon. That meant it was almost time. Weston squinted into the dirty sky. That meant—

The siren.

It rose, blaring out over the valley, a deafening drone that was unforgiving.

Everyone stopped what they were doing. The preacher's voice trailed off, and he lowered his head. Even the Constable was not immune to the siren's authority. Through the siren's blare, Weston thought he heard Annabeth's voice. *"You're falling so far away . . ."*

With his hands still bound, he lifted the noose from around his neck and jumped off the box. He scrambled off the platform and was kicking up dirt below before the Constable or anyone else could react. He tore through the street back to the jail, where they had moved his horse. He pulled his hands free from the rope. He untied his mare, climbed atop, and kicked into her sides desperately. "Ride, girl," he croaked into her ear. He saw no sign of the Constable or his deputies behind him, but he knew they wouldn't be long. He blew through the town like a bullet and headed straight for the mountain.

He headed up the pass and rode hard until it was too steep for his steed. He jumped off and continued on foot, using rocks and sparse trees as handholds. He climbed and searched, and almost gave up, until he saw something glint in the sun. Around a bend, he saw a door.

It was unlike any door he had ever seen. It was metal, but it was too smooth. It had a shine to it that was unnatural. It had no handle. He stepped to it and put his hands against its surface, recoiling at how cold it felt. To its side was a button that was lit, as if a small lantern were hidden inside it. Weston considered it for a moment, touched it with a shaky finger and jumped back when the door slid open. He hesitated and then walked inside.

What he saw next, he didn't understand.

A large chamber inside the mountain was lit as bright as the sun. It was all white and silver, the walls and floor made of metal. The room was lined with . . . something. Like mirrors, only they held pictures of the town below, and some just words, and numbers, and shapes. Everything had lights—blue, red, yellow. There was a large console in the center of the room, with still more lights and panels.

Beyond the door was a large chamber. Its walls were metal, polished to an unnatural shine. From behind this, a man stepped out.

"Y-you're not supposed to be here!"

Barely a man, he was young, with short black hair, a long white coat buttoned to the top, and a look of absolute terror on his face.

"What are you doing? You need to go back to the town!"

Weston eyed him well. "What is this place?" His head had calmed, but it was taking all his effort to understand what he was seeing.

"It's nothing! A dream!" said the man, though the fright in his voice betrayed him. Then to himself, but loud enough for Weston to hear: "I knew it was just a matter of time before one of you became immune to it."

Weston leaped at him, putting his hand around the man's throat and pinning him against the wall. A screen behind the man's head glowed. Like the moon. Like fireflies in a bottle. Weston didn't like it.

"You will tell me what is happening right now or I will crush your windpipe, do you understand me?" These words were carried on a growl and felt foreign coming out of Weston's mouth. He felt his actions being driven by something else deep inside him.

"F-fine! Okay! I'm a scientist! I'm just a scientist!" the man said in a rushed, shaky voice.

Weston had heard this word before. It had a vague meaning, something to do with the distant past. He didn't like this, either. He lessened his grip on the scientist's throat.

"You're . . . Weston, right?"

Weston nodded slowly. "How do you know my name?"

The man pointed to one of the screens. "We've been monitoring the town. I'm a scientist. And I'm just trying to help you! You're in danger! Or, you *were* in danger. We saved you!"

Weston released his grip entirely and took a step back. "There's more of you?" he asked, looking around.

"Not anymore. The others, they . . . died." The

answer came weakly, almost too silent to hear. "There's just me now."

An uncomfortable silence followed. And then:

"What sort of danger?"

"An explosion."

"Nothing's blown up here as long as I can remember," Weston said with a dubious glance.

"No. Not yet. It hasn't happened yet, but we could see it. It would've killed us all, us and the entire town. The entire valley!"

"Okay," Weston said, signaling he wanted more.

"Look, we stopped time just before the explosion. We stopped it before it could—"

"Stop . . . time?" Weston had a hard time with these words together.

"Yes. That was our main area of study here. Time manipulation. We were trying to find a way back. Back before the world fell apart. Our experiments failed. This . . . energy was building up, and it was going to be catastrophic. But we stopped it from happening—at least for us, so that we could find a way to prevent it. We're in a time loop. Every six days, we go back."

"Time loop?" Weston shook his head as if this was a dream he could shake away. "I don't understand."

"Okay," said the scientist, his confidence slowly returning. "Picture horses running in a straight line. Just like time. Now if you put those horses in a corral? And they keep on running. They run from one point, around in a circle, until they come back to that original point."

Weston took a moment, but nodded. "Okay," he said slowly.

"We essentially did the same thing with time. We corralled it. And it takes us six days to go all the way around the corral. On the seventh day, the world would've ended."

"We don't remember any of this, but you do?"

"Time travel is tricky. The physical world resets, but our consciousness, well, that's something that eludes even our science. It transcends everything. It stays with us. That's where the siren comes in. It erases your memories. Makes them fuzzy, at least."

Weston frowned. "So we don't remember what we've done the week before. To us it's always the week after you put us in this, ah, corral."

"Yes! You've got it!"

Weston shook his head furiously. "Why would you do this?"

"Well, we thought—some of the other scientists believed, that is—that you would all go mad. Living the same few days over and over again." Then he added softly, looking away to a corner of the room. "They were right." He paused, giving this statement an unimaginable weight, and when his eyes returned, they were glassy. "And anyway, we had hoped to find a way to fix it before any of you knew what was happening."

"Just . . . how long have we been doing this?"

The man went flush. "I honestly lost track. Fifty or sixty, maybe."

"Days?"

"Years."

Weston stumbled backwards, and caught himself on the center console. *You're falling further away from me.*

"So you see, the siren—the *signal*—it was imperative to keep the peace. So you wouldn't remember before. Or what was left behind. We thought we were getting close, but then the other two died." The scientist looked very uncomfortable. "I've been alone for so long. I don't think I can fix it! I can't do any of this on my own!" He was pleading now, his voice on the edge of collapse.

Weston cocked his head. "What do you mean, *what was left behind?*"

"Well," the scientist began, shakily again, "not everyone made it into the time loop. The radius of our generator. It covered most of the valley, but not all of it."

"Who was left behind?"

"We did everything we could, we couldn't save everybody!" He was pleading again.

"*Who was left behind?*" Weston shouted in rage, both hands now back at the scientist's throat.

"Lots of people." The scientist looked away, knowing there was only one name Weston wanted. He added reluctantly, "Annabeth. The pox, it was just a memory we put in you. We thought we were helping!" The scientist's body collapsed. "I'm so sorry."

Weston stormed forward again, his face looming over the scientist's. His voice was frantic. "Can you take me back to her? Can I be with her again?"

"I can't! If we leave the loop, we'll all die! The explosion will kill us all! We're trapped!"

Weston fell back again, this time to the ground.

The scientist pressed his head to the floor, repeating "I'm so sorry" quietly, like an incantation to right all wrongs.

Weston's head began thrumming again. It felt swollen and ready to explode. The thing that was trying to crawl out of his memory was finally succeeding. He felt then that he could almost see her face, her true face, in the distance and reaching out to him as something shimmered between them. She was getting smaller and smaller, crying, reaching out to him. A longing suddenly grew inside him, black and overwhelming, weakening his legs and bringing him to his knees. Tears poured over his face.

"I'd rather die with Annabeth," he growled, "than live one more second in your godforsaken loop." He spotted a metal bar off to the side, grabbed it, and with no hesitation started smashing the panels around him. Sparks flew and alarms blared as he delivered blow after blow, exposing cables and ripping them out with his hands.

The scientist screamed "No, you don't understand! We'll just be stranded in time! NO!" but in the end he didn't have the willpower to do anything but sit on the ground and sob into his hands. "It doesn't matter anyway. I'm sorry, I'm so sorry."

All the tiny lights went out, and the alarms stopped. Weston dropped the metal bar to the floor, a clang echoing loudly. Weston left the chamber in a daze. He shuffled down the mountain, found his horse, and rode back into town slowly.

He went to the saloon, walked inside and took a seat next to Gideon. Bennett greeted him casually.

Weston looked him over, and also Gideon, who was deep in drink. He hesitated, then asked, "Any news of the Constable?"

"Haven't seen him for a day or so. No Constable is a good Constable, if you ask me," Bennett said with a wink.

They'd all forgotten. When the siren blared, as he ran. The fight. The hanging. None of it had ever happened.

Some small relief flushed through him. Then he dared to ask his next question. His lips felt dry and cracked, and did not want to move. Finally, "And what of Annabeth?"

Bennett frowned and offered Weston a consoling look. "A pity."

Those two words made Weston's heart drop. He

knew the chances were small, but some part of him hoped, *prayed*. She was gone now, some sixty years away in a whole different world. He left without a word, rode home slowly, and lay down. Sleep took him again.

That night, there were no dreams.

He awoke the next day, rode out to the old rusty pump, and filled his water skin.

At noon, he waited for the siren, but it did not come. He marked a line in the ground.

He repeated this every day, and every day afterwards. On the seventh day, he saw his lines were gone. He fell to his knees, and the dirt soaked up his tears.

The days grew into months. The months into years.

Learning the truth, the townspeople stormed the mountain. The scientist hung from the gallows until he was dust and bones. It changed nothing. Some of them gave up, some went mad.

At high noon every day, Weston Holt looked to the mountain and cursed. And longed for that siren.

Here's a happy little tale from Charles Godfrey. It's called . . .

THE SEVEN GATES OF HELL

By Charles Godfrey

It began one dark winter night in York County, while I was driving to work. Earlier it had snowed and there was a light dusting on the ground.

I was on Trout Run Road when, in my rearview, I spotted a truck approaching. The truck got up on my bumper, and I saw men in the back flailing their arms, drinking beer, and hollering. It looked like a truckload of hillbillies. My first thought was *The Hills Have Eyes* movie had come true and that I was going to die. But after a few hair raising minutes, they went around me, laughing. One threw his beer can at me. *It hit my car, the bastard.*

Suddenly, the car's engine quit and I rolled to a stop. I pulled my cell phone from my pocket and went to call my boss, but the phone wasn't working. There were no bars in the upper left corner, no reception. I put the phone away and got out of the car. I figured I'd check under the hood for any obvious trouble. That's when I saw a body lying prone on the side of the road. Something inside me said, *Get back in the car.* You know, that feeling in your gut when you sense danger, but can't really see it. But I figured, *A man's life is at stake here.* So I walked over to see if I could help.

"Are you okay?" I asked.

It was a young man, black hair, wearing a brown jacket. He mumbled something unintelligible. I shook his shoulder to check his response.

"Please don't kill me," he managed to say.

I felt instant sorrow. "I'm not here to kill you. What happened?"

"A pick-up truck full of kids just ran me down."

He tried to roll over, so I helped him onto his back. The whole time he was in pain and gasping for air. His face was scratched and bleeding. He had thick blood coming from his nose.

"I'm a paramedic, I'm here to help you."

"No! Don't hurt me," he begged.

"At least let me get you to the hospital."

"No! I can't go back!"

"Back where?" I asked.

He didn't answer.

"So where would you like to go—home?" I asked.

"Yes, take me home."

"Where's home?"

He pointed to the woods down the road. I got up to have a look. I felt the cold wind down my neck and pulled up my collar. The road took a sharp turn to the left a hundred feet up ahead. There also was a crush and run drive that went off to the right. That seemed strange since I had traveled Trout Run Road for the last month and had never seen that crush and run driveway.

"Help me to my feet," the man said.

I turned around and gave him a hand up. He put his arm around my shoulder and we started to walk toward the crush and run. I noticed he was hunched over. His back seemed deformed.

"Let me see if my car will start. If it does, we can take my car."

"No. It's just up the road," he said. "I'd rather walk."

When we got to the driveway, I looked up at the road sign. It read: "Toad Road."

"That's strange. Isn't this Trout Run Road?" I asked.

"They changed the name. I'm just up the road," the man said.

It was a cold winter night and the weatherman had said there was a chance of more snow. *I have to help him get home so he doesn't freeze to death.*

"A man in your condition. You sure you don't want me to get my car? It's right there."

"I'll be fine when I get home," the man said. "Please, it's not far."

We started up the gravel road. There were strange noises in the woods like children playing, laughing in the distance. The wind whistled past my ears and I saw shadows moving between the trees. The tree limbs hung low and seemed to reach out for me. Nothing seemed to bother my companion as I helped him walk. Just then a tree branch whipped my face.

"Ouch! That hurt." I felt my face and it was wet. "Damn branch cut my face."

The man didn't seem to care, he pulled me to keep walking. He really seemed to take the noises in stride. Believe you me, I thought about turning around, but I was helping him, so I continued. About a quarter-mile up the road we came to a fence with a gate.

"What do we have here?" I said.

"Just swing the gate open," the man said. "It's not locked."

As I did, the area ahead became a dark, dense woods. The crush and run became little more than a bridle path. I felt my body get tired when I went through.

"I feel better already," the man said.

"Are you sure?" I asked. He did seem to look better. The scratches on his face were just deep, dark wrinkles now. There was no blood. He must have wiped his face off.

I went to help him walk and he held his hand out to stop me. "I can walk."

We walked together for a while, but there was a strange ghostly sound coming from the woods, like someone moaning. Then I smelled burning. Not the good smell of wood, but the nasty smell—like when a house burns, roof shingles mixed with electric wiring burning.

I had to stop. "What's that sound?"

"Just the wind," the man said. "Don't worry, I own this property and I hear strange noises out here all the time. It's nothing."

"What about that smell?"

"The fireplace," he said.

It wasn't a fireplace sort of smell. "You sure it's not your house?"

Again, he ignored the question. I didn't see a glow in the distance and he wasn't worried and I was getting caught up in the journey. We walked another quarter-mile and there stood two white pillars.

"We need to pass through this gate," he said.

"How many gates do you have?" I asked.

"Just be sure to pass between the pillars," the man said.

"Why?"

"It's safer."

"Safer from what?"

He continued through the gateway. My curiosity was heightened, so I followed. Once past the pillars, the man's back straightened and he walked more normally. I tried examining him, but he pushed my hands away and I felt my life drain from me.

"I'm just making sure you're okay."

"I feel much better now. I'm invigorated just

being near home."

Feeling tired, I said, "You look okay now. Do you think you can get yourself home from here?"

"Oh, please walk with me. I haven't had company for so long."

"But I need to get to work."

"Your car is broken down, and I have a phone you can use."

"That's great. Where?"

"At the house."

"How much farther?"

"See that light in the distance?" He pointed.

"Yes. I do."

"That's my house."

His house was closer than my car, so I went with him. Making it through the dense cold woods was a chore. Low lying branches smacked my face again. I had defensive wounds all over my hands. We walked until we came to a stream. Then I thought I saw weird lights zip through the woods.

"What's that?" I said.

"Fireflies," he answered. "Nothing to worry about."

Fireflies in the winter? I don't think so. More like orbs.

He showed me where to cross. It was a tree that had fallen across the creek.

"Are you sure it's safe?"

"If I can do it, so can you."

When I stepped onto the log, a dense fog set in over the water. It swirled around my feet, and I felt it caress my ankles. I bolted across that log to the other side, slipped, and went head first into the cold mud.

"You okay?" the man asked.

I stood and wiped my face. The front of me was covered with icy mud. He started up a hill and I followed. At the top of the hill we came to a cemetery.

"A cemetery? Out here?"

"My family plot," the man said.

"Is it much farther? Because I don't think I can go much farther, and I don't see your house."

He looked out across the way and pointed. "There. Can you see that light?"

The light was just as far away as the last time he pointed to it.

Suddenly, I heard dogs barking and the rustling of the ground cover. "What's that about?" I asked.

"Run! We need to go through the cemetery," the man said.

It was cold. I couldn't feel my toes any longer. And I bolted for my life. I followed him into the cemetery. Once inside, the howling stopped.

"Where'd they go?" I asked, panting.

"They can't come in here."

"Can't, or won't?"

I walked carefully, trying not to step on the graves of the dead. I felt it disturbed them. On the far side I saw a woman hanging. She was hung! In a tree!

"You see that?" I said. "Quick—we need to help her!"

I ran toward her. I tripped and almost fell, but I managed to stay on my feet. When I got closer, no one was there.

"Where'd she go?" I turned around and behind me was a little girl dressed in white. I was startled and went backwards, then fell on my butt. The hair on the back of my neck stood up.

"Turn around and go back," she said.

The man came up and chased her away. But instead of running, she disappeared.

"Did you see that?" It was obvious he saw.

"Why'd you do that?" I asked.

"She's dangerous. We must get out of the cemetery," he said.

"What about the dogs?"

He grabbed me by the wrist and directed me to the other end of the cemetery.

"Stop! I want to go home now," I cried.

"You want to go home. Go ahead. No one is stopping you. You think you can get to your car with those dogs out there, go right ahead. Why do you think those dogs are out there? They roam these woods in search of something to eat." He seemed to have regained all his strength, and his voice was strong and forceful.

He opened the gate and walked me out. I had no willpower, I was drained and exhausted. I found myself in an open field. This was strange because it had been a dense forest just a second ago. Across the way stood a two-and-a-half-story Victorian house with a wraparound front porch. Its front door glowed red.

"There it is."

This guy had strung me along, and now I couldn't go back. Fear had set in. Fear of getting lost going back alone. Fear of those dogs getting me. My only choice now was to get to the safety of the house and call for help.

He led me across the field of tall grass. That's when I noticed the man I was with walked briskly and erect. When he got to the house he turned to me. He looked older. His face had a grayish color and he had lost his deformity.

"I do hate this part so," the man muttered.

"What part?"

"Free will," he said. "You must choose to enter."

"This is your home, right?" I said.

"You are about to enter the seventh gate. You

have passed through six already."

"But I didn't go through six gates," I argued.

Now the man had an evilness about him. He looked me in the eyes and said, "Oh, yes—you did. You entered the first gate simply by touch.

"The second gate is invisible. You entered it when you stepped onto Toad Road.

"The third gate was the fenced-in area.

"The fourth gate was the two pillars.

"The fifth gate was when you entered the cemetery. The girl tried to warn you."

"You son of a — " I bit my tongue. His eyes pierced my very soul. He continued.

"The sixth gate was when you left the cemetery. You should feel proud of yourself. Not many make it to the seventh gate. Most only make it to the fourth or fifth before they die." He belted out a huge, sinister laugh.

"Who are you?"

He smiled. "Now we stand at the seventh gate, visible only at night. It's the front door to this house. You now have two choices. Choose to enter—or choose to die. Your choice."

With all the strength I had left, I turned and ran as fast as my feet could carry me. Back through the cemetery and out the other side. I tumbled down the hill and ran back across the log across the creek, through the two pillars, through the fence gate. Those dogs were nowhere to be found. I made it to the road and collapsed, bleeding profusely from my head and nose.

I was near death and felt an awful blackness come over me. I wanted to scream, but all that came from my mouth was a dreadful moan; then pitch black.

When I awoke, I was lying prone on the side of the road. A car was driving by. Suddenly, the car's engine shut off.

The driver got out of the car. It was a young woman. She came over to me and shook my shoulder.

"Are you all right?" she asked.

"Please don't kill me," I managed to say.

"I'm not here to kill you. What happened?"

Family is the best part about life. It's also the worst.

FLESH AND BLOOD

By Sharon Broomall

"It's a boy!"

Jack burst into the waiting room, arms raised, face flushed with triumph. He began working the small crowd like only he could, shaking hands, slapping backs and taking the same.

He reached for my hand, trying to mask his surprise. By rote I extended my arm, pressing my flesh to his. I had prayed this day would never come.

My brother's eyes met mine. "I've changed, Michael," he said. "Everything's changed." His remarks were slow and deliberate, despite the charge in the room.

I searched his face for a shadow of insincerity as he released me from his grip. I saw none, only a flicker of something I didn't recognize.

"I need to talk to Kat," I said.

I hadn't come to offer congratulations. I had come to shatter the silence that had stood between Jack and me for two decades.

* * *

I remember the smell of earth and rotting leaves and the metallic taste of blood in my mouth, the warmth of it running down my throat as I waited for what came next.

I swallowed the blood, and fear welled in its place.

* * *

The ground rumbled beneath me where I lay on a bed of crisp brown leaves. A cloudless autumn sky stretched above the rooftops of the shops and restaurants up the hill along Lancaster Avenue. Midmorning sun peeked over D'Angelo's Market, warming my face and glinting off the train tracks.

Jack scrambled up the embankment and pulled a handful of coins from his pocket. He jingled them in his fist, then opened his hand and laid them on the track, adding them to the half dozen already arranged in a line on the far rail.

The trembling of the ground intensified. Train cars clacked in the distance.

Jack laid down the nickels, dimes, pennies, and quarters, one by one, hand steady.

"Get down, Jack," I called. "The train's coming."

The cars had made their way around the bend. Jack stood between the rails in his Levi's and plaid flannel shirt, his eyes fixed on the single headlight of the engine as it sped toward him.

The tracks shuddered.

He ran his hand through his sun-bleached hair, reached into his pocket and yanked out two bottle caps and a half-dollar.

"Jack, the train!"

The commuter cars barreled at him. The whistle sounded, three long blasts. The train hissed as the engineer braked, too late.

"Jump!" I yelled.

The locomotive was nearly on top of him, horn blaring.

In one swift motion, Jack placed the half-dollar

on the rail, tossed the bottle caps aside, and dove off the tracks, rolling down the embankment.

He came to a halt next to me, covered in bits of dead leaves. He brushed away a twig that hung from his hair.

Fire consumed the sea green of his eyes. His ruddy cheeks glowed.

He grinned. "Think I scared him, Mikey?"

* * *

The cement steps were cold. A shiver went through me, and my hands shook. My nose throbbed from where I'd been punched. I wiped blood from my nostril.

Light seeped through the gap beneath the metal double doors, letting in a world I wished I could erase myself from.

In my mind I saw what lay outside—late-morning sun on red and gold mums that stretched to the sidewalk from the side yard, a close-cropped expanse of green; bags of raked leaves neatly lining the curb. I heard faint voices—Mom talking gardens and tennis with Mrs. Drayer over the backyard fence, laughing her country-club laugh, our neighbor skipping rope in her driveway, singing "Cinderella, Dressed in Yellow." A dog barked in the distance.

The metal doors flew open.

"Heeeeere's Johnny!"

Sunlight flooded in, blinding after 20 minutes in darkness. I wondered why it had taken him so long to find me this time.

* * *

A white truck with a cornucopia on the side roared up the alley that ran behind D'Angelo's and the other stores along the pike. Jack and I reclined in the leaves, lobbing osage oranges at nearby tree trunks. We watched as a man in a red cap backed the truck to the rear of the market, jumped from the driver's seat, and hustled in the entrance. A few minutes later he began unloading his cargo—crates and boxes of tomatoes, lettuce, and onions.

"Jack, let's go home. I'm getting hungry."

"Not yet."

When the storeroom of D'Angelo's had filled up, the man stacked boxes next to the ramp and dumpster out back.

The man hopped in his truck. The engine groaned to a start, and he drove off.

Jack flipped his flattened half-dollar in the air. "Heads or tails?"

"Heads."

"Heads—you lose. Come on," he said, motioning toward D'Angelo's.

"Where are we going?" I called.

His words tumbled downhill as he crested the embankment. "It's time to make vegetable soup."

Jack had already ripped into one of the boxes by the time I reached the alley. "Ten tons of steel meets ten pounds of tomatoes. Sounds like fun, doesn't it?"

"What if someone catches us?"

"Don't be a nerd." He surveyed the crates piled around us. "What the heck—why not make it twenty pounds? Take this box. I'll grab that one over there," he said, pointing to a tomato carton on top of a stack behind the dumpster. He disappeared to get it.

"OK." I bent to tie the lace of my Puma.

There was a tap on my shoulder.

"Whadaya think you're doing, Clifton?"

I looked up to see Billy Butler's silver-capped front tooth gleaming in the sun. Stevie D'Angelo, standing by Billy's side in his striped rugby shirt, stared at me through Coke-bottle lenses.

"Uh . . . nothing," I muttered as I stood, heart slamming against my ribs.

Billy Butler was the biggest, meanest, oldest kid at Radnor Elementary. He was in the sixth grade with Jack, but only because he'd been held back twice. He stood a half-foot taller than Jack and outweighed him by 30 pounds. It was widely known that Billy had a crush on his chesty 13-year-old half-sister.

"We're having a little snack, asshole," said Jack, appearing from behind the dumpster.

"Is that right." Billy turned to his sidekick, half his size. "This is your Dad's cousin's uncle's store, ain't it, Stevie?"

"Yeah. Something like that." Stevie kicked at stones on the pavement.

Billy inched closer to me, and my heart hammered harder. I smelled lunchmeat on his breath. "So if these dipshits are stealing from your Dad's cousin's uncle, they're stealing from you, right?"

"That's kind of a stretch, but—"

Billy elbowed Stevie.

"Yeah, sure they are," Stevie said.

"That's a good reason for me to pound them into the ground, ain't it?"

"Uh-huh," Stevie agreed.

Billy grabbed the collar of my polo shirt, pulled back his fist, and prepared to let fly.

Jack hurtled himself at Billy, knocking him off balance and sending him tumbling into his sidekick. Stevie and his glasses were thrown to the macadam. Billy's punch landed on my nose, but it was a softer blow than it would have been if Jack hadn't tackled him.

I reached instinctively to my face, stunned from the punch. Down the embankment, the tracks began to rumble as another commuter car made its way down the Main Line.

"My glasses! He broke my glasses!" Stevie cried, reaching for his tortoiseshell frames, now missing a lens.

Unsteady from the pounding in my head, I swung at Billy.

Jack grabbed my fist before it met Billy's chin. Rage flashed in Jack's eyes.

My arm fell to my side as Jack picked up Stevie's lens from the blacktop. The clatter of the approaching train grew louder.

Jack pointed down the alley, behind Billy. "Billy, look! It's your sister and she's stark fucking naked!"

Billy spun around.

Jack hurled the lens toward the tracks and signaled for me to run.

The train roared by. I sprinted the six blocks home to Devon Avenue.

* * *

"Your nose is bleeding," Jack said. "We better go inside and check that out." He grabbed my arm and yanked me up the concrete steps. "Good thing I was there to block Billy's punch, huh?"

Yeah, and to block mine.

He pulled me in the front entrance of the house. The storm door slammed behind us.

"I don't need you to look at my nose. I'll take care of it. If I want help, I'll get Mom."

My face throbbed, but the pain didn't matter. All I felt was the leaden sickness in my gut. Knowing what Jack would do. Knowing I couldn't stop it. And knowing I was somehow at fault.

"Shut up and walk. You know the game. I do something for you, you do something for me." He shoved me up the stairs. "If it weren't for me, you'd be lying in your own piss behind D'Angelo's."

He pulled me into Mom and Dad's bathroom. The lock on the hall bathroom door never worked.

Everything in me told me to run. But I didn't listen to myself anymore.

He closed the door behind us. The deadbolt slid home, metal on metal.

The rest is only flashes of memory—shards of broken images, razor-sharp sensations that rise from the blackness and pierce my consciousness.

Jack's hands on me. Jack covering my mouth as I stare down at the black-and-white tile and wait for it to be over. Jack's voice in my ear, threatening that no one will believe me if I tell. That I'll be worse off if I do.

My mind can't remember any more.

My heart still burns with hatred.

* * *

"Meet your nephew," Jack said, taking a seat on the hospital bed next to his wife.

Katherine's face, still damp with perspiration from childbirth, glowed with the brilliance of the sun streaming through the window. An antiseptic scent betrayed the homeyness of the room.

Katherine whispered so she wouldn't wake the baby in her arms, wrapped in a blanket the same hue as the June sky. "I'm glad you came. We didn't think . . ."

"I needed to be here," I said, louder than I'd intended. Blood pulsed in my ears.

Jack smoothed a strand of Katherine's dark hair and stretched his arm around her and the baby. His eyes came to rest on mine, and he held me firmly in his gaze, imploring.

I've changed. Everything's changed.

I turned to the window, my insides taut. "I came to tell you something," I said to the horizon, weighing the burden of our poisoned youth, the duty it now pressed upon me, and Jack's words in the waiting room.

"We need to tell you something, too," Katherine said.

My eyes returned to her face and the promise in her arms.

"We named the baby Michael," Jack said.

Talk about a tough neighborhood to deliver newspapers . . .

THE HOUSE

By Bob Knapp

The sky above me at 4 a.m. is a black-painted dome speckled with white dots. Well below it, a hazy light dims to near darkness. A smattering of street lamps atones for the missing moon. The late October wind sighs in treetops and runs its icy fingers beneath my coat. An occasional dry leaf floats to the ground. I am sailing newspapers onto porches, as I do every day but Sundays.

I notice none of this; dread preoccupies me.

The three hundred customers' houses are like clones—old bungalows with deep porches across the front of the house, sitting wide, two stories high but looking squat, buried in the shadows of their trees and bushes. But the exception strangles my mind, even though I keep telling myself that it is exactly like the other brown, shake-covered houses.

Robot-like, I pull a paper from the bundle resting in a strap hung from my shoulder, fold the paper, and fling it onto the next porch. There is a plop and then a skittering sound as it slides across the wooden floor. I see it settle next to the door. Except for the falling leaves and me, there is no other movement—not even a cat.

I try to think about everything else: how my pay, ten dollars per week, is better than most teenagers earn and wonder why the previous paperboy quit— or disappeared, as rumored. I try to dwell upon my senior classes, Friday's Halloween party, getting my driver's license, graduating this school year: 1958. I imagine I am talking with the blonde who sits next to me in English, but even her image fades. Fear of the house pushes away all thoughts, save of it. Ordinarily, the rustle of fallen leaves about my feet soothes, but I hear nothing.

Repeatedly, I tell myself that nothing about the house should alarm me. I have received no harm, not even a threat. Why worry or care? Like the other houses, I have never seen its occupants. In seconds, I will have delivered its paper and be past it—safely. But always upon passing this house an image of a beautiful girl, beckoning to me, appears. I have assumed that it is an adolescent fantasy, but the vision never occurs anywhere but there. I cannot willfully conjure it up. There is a reasonable explanation, is there not? Perhaps it is some past acquaintance, or passerby, and these surroundings remind me of it.

I'm painstakingly aware that I am drawing nearer the house. In spite of the cold, my underarms dampen, moisture forms on my upper lip, the hair on my neck is wet, and I'm not even on the house's street. In mornings past, had it not been for my pride, I would have crossed to the other side of the street and not delivered a paper. Anyone who would have seen me would have thought me a coward.

I see the house now. My pulse races and pounds in my ears—what foolishness. Today, I'll prove there is nothing to fear from the house and get over this nonsense. The house looms large. Chills creep down my back and legs. My hands tingle. A rock enters my stomach; my legs are feeble snakes.

The house sits in mid-block where another street ends into it, making a 'T'. The house dominates the houses surrounding it. Thankfully, a streetlight illuminates this intersection. It does me little good. Strangely, although there is nothing between it and the light, the house appears dark, as if in the deepest shadow. No reflection from window glass. *Black on black, on a black night, I think. Why did I assume the house was brown?* Somehow, the porch seems even a deeper black.

I shudder. I'm cold from sweat running down my back, dampening my clothes.

Perhaps the blackness of this house is my imagination. I make sure the newspaper is lock-folded tight. No excuse for a missing thud as it lands on the porch—like maybe it opened and floated down to the floor. I hurl the paper toward the porch, but wait and watch, as if this is a test. I listen extra-long, straining my ears, for the thud.

Nothing.

The hair on my neck stands straight up. Chills run up and down my spine. I should walk on, but I've sworn to myself that I will not.

Before you investigate, try another paper, I tell myself. I fold and throw the newspaper, this time higher, with the right touch so that it will fall hard on the porch deck. The paper disappears into silence.

What I really want to do is run. I tremble. I force my first step toward the house, and then another step and another, until I am there. I raise my legs to where I think the stair steps are located until I reach what seems to be the porch floor. I expect it to feel soft or covered with a deep rug, but the steps and floor are hard—that is, of normal consistency. I look for a paper, thrown, I am sure, to the base of the door. I strain to see my own feet. I place each foot down, one after the other, as if to avoid stepping off into a deep void, yet I expect to brush a newspaper at any time. I should have inched far enough forward by now to have reached the door, so I bend to feel for a paper.

At that moment, there is a change in the air. Looking up, I see that the door is open to an unbelievably darker doorway. In it stands a man, blacker than any person I have ever seen. Actually, I can barely see him, although instinctively I know he is Caucasian, like me. I am so startled I barely keep myself from collapsing onto the floor.

"Nice toss," he says. "I didn't have to move an inch. Come in, you must be terribly cold." He sniffs the papers and lets out a contented "Ahh." I discern that he is gesturing with them for me to come inside.

I'm not cold, but then remember that I really am. I am able to straighten up but my feet absolutely will not move until he takes me gently by the arm and pulls so that I must step forward so not to lose my balance. Once inside, he asks, "Would you like a hot cup of black coffee? I must apologize, we do not have cream."

I manage to stutter that I have not yet begun drinking coffee. "A nice cup of hot cocoa, then. Melanie will come to entertain you. I must get ready for my patients—the Wilmer Eye Clinic at Johns Hopkins—night shift." It is settled before I can answer.

He offers me a seat and a place to drop my newspapers on what seems a void, but I assume it is a black sofa, and then he is gone. In the blackness of the room, I am having trouble discerning objects. I have the impression that persons are moving about, but I cannot really see anyone. I then realize I cannot see my own body. I pat my chest to make sure that I actually exist. I must be dreaming. I struggle to wake up.

Formerly, I had been frightened by this house without real cause. Now, in spite of the hospitality which is being granted me, I am terrified. My mind races—the one good thought I have is to bolt for the door—if indeed I can find it. They are all blind and have no need for light, I reason.

I feel the sofa give way next to me. Someone has seated himself or herself next to me, quite close, actually. "Hi, I'm Melanie," she says as she puts her hand on my near shoulder and leans her body against mine to let me know she is there. Although she appears as black as the sofa, I am learning to discern differences. Her breath is warm and carries a pleasant odor. I choose to believe she is actually blonde and quite lovely. She attempts to engage me in conversation to help me relax, but it is not working. I suddenly realize that she is actually the same girl I have been visualizing since taking this newspaper job. I tremble violently. I try to arise but I am so weak that she belays me simply by placing her hand on my arm.

"You needn't be afraid of us. We are very happy that you have come. And I know you very well," Melanie says.

I say nothing. My words might be used against me.

"I've been watching you deliver the papers. You are very conscientious, among other attributes." Her manner gives the impression that she is years older than me. "Kind, considerate, industrious. Handsome," she adds. It seems like she is reciting from a check-off list.

Warmth to my neck and my cheeks displaces my chills. She pulls away slightly. "I'm sorry to have embarrassed you." She must have some power to read my mind.

A man is suddenly standing near us. I think I

have acquired the senses of a blind person, too. I realize that he holds a steaming cup. "I did not introduce myself to you," he says. "I am Jack, Melanie's father."

I think, *Black Jack,* as I sip the very dark cocoa. Melanie giggles. That proves she can read my thoughts. How can I control what I think?

He waits, and I think he is wondering what else to say. "That's all right, we already know your name," he says at last.

I'm embarrassed again. He was waiting for me to introduce myself. I offer my hand to shake and he grabs it immediately, as if it is full daylight. "Oh, I'm—"

"Jerry, isn't it?" he says before I can tell him. "We'll be having supper soon. Would you care to join us? Pardon, me, it would be breakfast time for you.

"We make very good use of your paper," Jack says. "In fact, I was very pleased that you delivered two. Really, the papers have been small of late, and we have had to dip into our reserves." I knew he was staring at me. "We could use your entire bundle, although it is better if we have fresh news each day."

I had no idea what to make of this. Finally, I find my tongue and I say only what I know to be true. "My other customers are expecting their papers. In fact, I really must go." I am curious, but too fearful of this family to find out more. They probably are using the papers to house train a pack of pups. I had not seen nor heard them, but by now, that is no surprise to me. I stand, expecting to be shown to the front door.

"We don't read the paper, but we do know what the articles say," Melanie says. "But the newspapers are essential to us. Let me show you." I weakly protest but she takes me by the hand and guides me toward the back of the house. To have such a beauty keep a close rein upon me is no unpleasant matter. The papers will be late, that's all. Chills of a pleasant sort course through my body, and then, as I think, *She may really be an old hag,* I am sick.

Through room after room she leads me, at least it seems that way as one door after another is opened and I am guided through their entryways. I am amazed at the house's size and wonder about the extent of their family.

Finally, we enter the rear room of the house where something bright, like a snow-covered hillside on a sunny day, blinds my eyes until they adjust. Newspapers without any writing on them are stacked in a pile. Amazingly, the papers are the source of light for this room. Immediately, I look at Melanie and see she is wearing overalls. She moves with the semi-awkwardness of a blind person, much as I had been just moments ago. Could it be that I could not see how awkward she is?

She feeds a normal printed newspaper from another pile into a black machine, then turns it on. It looks very much like the wringer from an old washing machine, but it makes a quiet humming sound not made by washers. As the paper exits this wringer, it is snow white. She adds it to the blazing white pile. Attached to the side of the wringer is a small cone shaped device. As I watch, black drops fall from the narrow end of the cone into a collecting bottle.

"Why not buy black ink?" I ask.

"We have tried that. It doesn't work."

"In fountain pens? That's what ink is for."

A long minute passes while she continues to feed the machine newspaper and collect the blank ones. I begin to wonder if she will respond; it's almost as if she did not hear me.

I realize I have been so astounded that I have

forgotten to note what Melanie really looks like. I take this opportunity in the light to look at her. Even though she is in overalls, I am far from disappointed. Her body pushes on the overalls in all the right places. Her face is oval and framed by black hair. Arching eyebrows frame large black eyes. Something is different about her eyes.

She realizes I am staring and quickly turns her eyes away. "There is so much to explain, I hardly know where to start." There is a short buzz, a signal, from the machine. "I almost forgot the bottle; it's full." Her hands find another machine and an opening in its top. She guides the top of the ink-filled collection bottle to the opening and pours the ink inside this machine. With measured steps she moves to a cabinet behind us, feels for a handle that I readily see, and pulls out a small drawer. It is laden with smaller bottles, vials really, some of which have already been filled and have a shiny cap on them.

My heart races. She is showing me how to make some kind of dope. That's why they keep it so dark. They're criminals! They don't want anyone to see them. Why do they want me? I have to get out of here!

Melanie removes a small tray holding about six of the vials. Returning to the second machine, she feels for and finds what looks like a mail slot, and then slides the tray through it into the machine. After a press of a button, there is the sound of steam under pressure and the escape of vapor. "Sterilizing them," Melanie says. There are loud simultaneous clicks. "That's the caps. They must cool a little."

It dawns on me that she really can't see in light, so they are training me to use this machine.

"Let's go back into this room where I can see,"

Melanie says. She opens a door and disappears into the darkness. I follow her in. Even as the door shuts slowly behind me, no light enters this room.

"Let's sit here," she says, and gently holding my upper arm, guides me to a soft seat. It seems to have no back. "You're trembling."

I know she wants an answer, but hardly know what to say. "I need to deliver my papers. And then get to school."

"We decided we needed to use your bundle of papers—sorry. This is more important. It's our life."

"But it's not my life! Delivering the papers is my life." Instantly, I regret my outburst. I realize it's because I'm afraid of what may happen. "I'm sorry, I didn't mean to yell."

She pats my arm. "That's okay. I understand. You will be fine. But you can't go yet."

At least she said 'yet.' I'm breathing fast and try to settle down. "Okay, but tell me what is going on. The ink—what's it for?"

"So we can see. You see how bright the paper gets when the ink is removed. Something in the paper comes out with the ink. It's the only kind of ink we can use."

"How can ink . . .?"

"S-h-h-h. Just listen. Our eyes don't work like yours. They have three slits in them, one vertical and two horizontal ones at the ends of the vertical slit, like the printed letter 'I'. "

I look above the source of her voice to try to see her eyes. I think I see two small red glowing lights.

"Yes, once you learn exactly where to look, you can see our pupils. They appear as a faint red rather than black like yours. Our eyes send out a beam, faster than the speed of light, examine what they are directed upon, and return to the eye—something like sonar. More is brought back than just an image.

That's why we like the 'Freshies,' the most recent news. If there is a match with what is already in our brains, it's built upon. If not, a new structure is started. It's really more complicated than that, but you get the idea."

"You drink the ink?" My stomach convulsed.

"Inject it with a hypodermic syringe. You remember the vials."

She wasn't asking me. I shuddered.

"So what do you want from me?" I was afraid of the answer so I quickly added, "In your house, I can't see a thing. I won't be of any use to you."

Melanie ignored my plea, except to give me another hug. I leaned away from her.

"We're already very dark, but the ink makes us blacker." I could feel her shrug. "That's just how we are. I'm sorry you are so nervous, Jerry. I'm not surprised—as I said, I know lots about you. When we say, 'I see,' it means we understand, we know, we have acquired—in the way of information—what is on the inside of whatever we look at. And the ink—a bonus—it has all that information."

"Then why . . .?"

"To communicate, we do not have to talk." She answered before I could finish. "But we enjoy talking—something left over from a previous time. Besides, we need to talk with outsiders so they know what we are thinking, and to train them."

Train?

"Oh," Melanie says. "I forgot. I'll try to remember to give you a chance to talk and ask questions. And my whole family agrees—you are 'The One.' "

I jump up. "The *one* what?" Frantically, I look around the room for a doorway, but can see nothing.

"Give me time to explain and you won't be sorry. Please don't be afraid." She reaches up, takes my arm and pulls me back to my seat. This time when she hugs me I feel her longing. She is trying to get me to do something I don't want to do.

"In the daylight, we are blind, you know—legally blind. People are so prejudiced; the blind have difficulty buying new houses, so we keep adding on as our family, our clan, grows. Yes, the house is huge. From front to back, ten rooms and two stories high. We ran out of property. All of our kin live here. Now there is no more room to grow. We will start a new clan in another neighborhood—wherever we can get a house."

She waits, looking at me, deciding—no— determining whether I understand. Blind? And I still don't understand where I fit into the picture.

"Besides, we need new blood or else . . ."

I zone out. It is hard to tell if you faint when everything around you is absolutely black. I realize I am crawling on the floor toward where I think there is a door. I hear her end a sentence with ". . . and we will die out with horrible diseases." They want to inject my blood so it will rejuvenate them, keep them alive.

Melanie sounds like she is coughing, but I realize she has her hand over her mouth to try to muffle her laughing. My head bumps into what I know are a pair of legs. Strong hands grasp me by the arms and raise me to my feet. Melanie gives up pretense and roars with laughter. A bass voice near my face joins hers. I feel the humor and am almost compelled to join them. But the horror of my situation turns my loss of self-control in another direction. "My blood! My blood?" I scream. It is my turn to clap my hand over my mouth. As I settle myself, I feel my neck and ears turn red with embarrassment.

"We would never do anything like drain you of

blood," the bass voice in front of me says. It is Jack speaking, Melanie's father. "Sorry, Jerry. I have been trying to get Melanie to choose her words more carefully." He backs me to my soft seat. I think it is a bed.

"This is your bedroom," Jack says. "Temporarily."

"My bedroom!" I scream and jump to my feet again. "You said I could leave."

Jack takes my arm. I feel a prick on my upper arm.

Melanie gently grasps my head to pull my ear to her lips and whisper, "*Our* bedroom." I collapse to the bed.

* * *

It is so bright; I realize that it is morning, late morning. I jump from bed. I'm late serving my newspapers! I've had a nightmare.

My jaw drops. This isn't my room. My skin, it looks so dark.

A familiar voice addresses me, "Good morning, Sleepy Head."

I turn toward the voice. Standing in a doorway is a most beautiful woman, darker than any I have ever seen. Melanie. Somehow, I know exactly what she is thinking: *The eye surgery was successful— and he's all mine.*

"It's five a.m., Sunday. Are you ready for supper?" I knew she would ask that.

This is the kind of story—and lead character—that once kept the pulps running. So perhaps it's not out of place to say, "Return with us now to those thrilling days of yesteryear," and enjoy . . .

PARKER WILEY AND THE AMAZONS

By Chris Vaughan

August 17, 1937

The *Periquito*'s deck heaved under Parker Wiley's feet and sent him careening into the guardrail. He clung on with white knuckles as the tramp steamer dipped into the wave's trough and started up the next swell. At six-foot-two and nearly two hundred pounds, the handsome young millionaire wasn't used to being tossed around like a rag doll.

The tropical storm had blown up out of nowhere less than seventeen hours out of Montevideo, where he'd hired the *Periquito* to transport his circus up to Belize for the next engagement on its South American tour. It was a decision he now regretted. The ship was over thirty years old, and her captain was a notorious drunk. Parker hoped the old man was sober for once, but he had to get to the bridge and find out. He clawed his way along the rail and prayed that his footing held.

"Parker!"

Had he heard his name? He looked back and could just make out a hunched figure in an oversized rain jacket, hugging the balustrade. There were less than ten yards of visibility through the torrential rain, but he knew it had to be *her*. "Sara? I told you to stay in the cabin!"

Sara Sera was Parker's latest love interest—an aspiring actress he'd met that March in Los Angeles. She was blonde and usually gorgeous, but right now she looked like a drowned rat. He had to get her back inside.

"Wait there!" Cursing under his breath, Parker started back to her, but the ship chose that instant to roll to starboard. Parker's weight shifted forward and he was only able to stay out of the drink by wrapping his legs around a rusty support rail. When the ship righted itself, Sara was gone.

"Sara!" Parker half ran, half pulled himself down to where she'd been. The ocean was too dark and choppy for him to see her, but he knew she'd gone overboard. He grabbed a life ring and dove into the Atlantic after her.

Parker went deep under, and it took all his strength of will not to lose his grip on the ring. Although they were in relatively warm waters, it still felt shockingly frigid. He waited for the feel of the boat pulling on the ring, but only felt himself sinking deeper into the darkness instead.

The ring wasn't attached to the ship. The attachment point on the superstructure had probably rusted away.

Parker kicked off his boots and began scissor kicking towards the surface. At least he hoped it was towards the surface; it was pitch black and Parker prayed his attitude hadn't changed since he'd hit the water.

For several long moments, it seemed he'd chosen incorrectly, but then he felt himself break the surface. He gratefully gulped lungfuls of air, then choked as salt water forced its way into his mouth and out his nose.

He forced his eyes open against the burning spray. "Sara!" He could barely hear himself over the storm. Something moved in the corner of his eye. Had he imagined it? He turned toward it and saw a quick flash of khaki gray in the gloom. Parker swam toward it with all his strength. "Sara! Hang on!"

Another wave pushed him under. Instead of fighting back to the surface, he forced himself forward—reaching out his right arm and stretching his fingertips. She had to be there!

His fingers brushed something hard but smooth. Oilskin? Sara's slicker? Parker clutched at the material and held on as he once again reached the surface. He laughed for joy when he saw her blonde hair, but her head lolled to the side lifelessly. She was unconscious—or worse. He couldn't tell.

Somehow he managed to get the life ring around her and tie its rope around her waist. The preserver could barely support their combined weight and floated just below the surface. Parker cradled Sara's head in the crook between his jaw and chest, trying to shield her from the tempest. "Hang on, doll! You'll be okay."

Parker screamed for help, but it was in vain. He watched the *Periquito*'s lights melt into the darkness, and then they were alone.

* * *

Parker felt the sun beating down on his neck. He opened his eyes and saw a long ribbon of white beach separating a lush tropical forest from gently rolling waves. The sound of wild birds and insects competed with the *rumble-whoosh* of the breakers. Costa Rica? Brazil? When had he gone there? The last thing he remembered—

Parker rolled over and sat up. Sara's head,

which had been resting on his buttocks, flopped into the surf. She jerked wildly, then pushed her head out of the water with a startled gasp. The *Periquito*'s life ring—still lashed to them—bobbed up and down in the surf.

"Parker?" Sara rasped. "Where are we?"

"I'm not sure," Parker said. He stood and brushed the sand from his shirt and trousers. The beach was deserted, as was the ocean all the way to the horizon, and the forest's canopy stretched as far as Parker could see like an undulating carpet. "Brazil, probably."

"Do you think there are any people around?"

"Probably." Parker helped Sara up. She still wore the oilskin jacket from the night before, the tattered remnants of her dress underneath. Her legs were naked, and her hair was a wild mess of tangles, but—God bless her—she still looked like a million bucks.

"Probably? What if there aren't?"

"Well, you always liked the beach."

Sara slugged him in the shoulder. "This is some time to be making jokes."

Parker massaged his arm where she'd punched him. "Well, we wouldn't be in this mess if you'd stayed in the cabin like I'd told you."

"Oh, yeah? Well, *I* wouldn't be in this mess if I'd stayed in L.A. instead of running off with you, like *my* friends told *me*."

Parker grinned. "See what you'd be missing?"

"Ha. Right now the only thing I'm missing is a drink. I'm parched."

Parker slipped out of the life ring's rope and handed it to her. "I'll go find the cabana boy. While I do that, do you think you can unknot this rope? It might come in handy."

"Aye, aye, Captain," Sara said, giving Parker a

mock salute.

He returned the gesture and started towards the tree line. As he walked, he checked his pockets and was relieved to find his trusty jackknife. There was also a waterlogged wad of cash in a gold money clip—about a grand. It was his walking around money, and it'd be kindling if they couldn't get back to civilization.

When he reached the trees, Parker found a coconut lying in the sand. He cut off its fibrous outer husk and managed to bore a hole in the tough inner shell using his knife and a convenient flat stone as a hammer. After drinking his fill, he found another coconut and took it back to Sara.

When Sara saw it, she wrinkled her nose in disgust. "Ugh, I hate coconut." Then she reddened and shot Parker an apologetic look. "Sorry, coconut milk would be lovely. Thank you, Parker."

Sara took a small sip, and her eyes opened wide in surprise. "This is delicious." She drained the rest in one long draught.

"Funny how almost dying enhances your senses," Parker said. "Food tastes better, flowers smell better, music sounds better..."

Sara gave Parker a lascivious grin and snuggled up to him. "What else is better?"

"I like the way you think, doll. Why don't we—"

Before Parker could complete his thought, he was interrupted by a strange cry from the jungle. It started deep and throaty, like the mating call of a hippopotamus, before drifting up into a higher register, like a trumpeting elephant, and ending in a drawn out series of clacks.

"What was that?" Sara asked.

Parker shook his head slowly. "I've never heard anything like it; maybe some big species of bird."

A second call, similar to the first but much

closer, rose from the forest.

"That doesn't sound like any bird I ever heard," Sara hissed.

"Stay here," Parker whispered. "I'll go take a look."

"You're not leaving me alone! I'm going with you."

"Fine, but keep it down."

Sara gave Parker a look that said he might as well have warned her not to stick her finger in a light socket. She held onto his left arm, and they both crouched down and crept toward the forest.

When they reached the top of the beach, Parker tried to peer as deeply into the foliage as possible, but, at best, he could only see about five or six feet before everything was in the shadows of the ubiquitous palm fronds and fern leaves. He could make out lots of webs in the trees—and he hated to think about the size of the spiders that wove them—but that was about it.

"Let's walk up the beach a ways and see if we spot anything," Parker suggested. The last thing he wanted was to enter the forest unarmed and with bare feet. Who knew what kind of fauna was waiting in there. The giant spiders might be the most innocent thing in there.

Sara didn't argue, and they started creeping along parallel to the forest. The visibility didn't improve, but at least they didn't hear any more vocalizations.

They hadn't gone far, though, when they stumbled upon something that made Parker's blood run cold. A series of animal tracks led out of the jungle ahead of them. The tracks stretched down the beach away from them before eventually disappearing back into the forest.

Whatever had made the tracks had three toes

and ran on two legs, like a rhea or other large bird, but much bigger. Parker knelt and put his hand in one of the prints. With his fingers splayed out, he could almost span the width of the middle toe, but not even a third of its length.

"Those look fresh," Sara whispered.

She was right. "I saw prints like these once in England," Parker said. "At the natural history museum. But the thing that made them has been extinct for millions of years."

"Parker, you're scaring me. What's been extinct for millions of years?"

"It was a dinosaur."

Sara guffawed. "A dinosaur? Next you'll be telling me there's a giant monkey around here looking for a date."

"You're right, that's crazy. It must be a large bird. That makes more sense. It's just got to be enormous." Parker frowned. "The bad news is, this means we're probably on an island—or a really remote part of the mainland. Otherwise everyone would know about these things."

"Well, since the tracks go that way," Sara said, "I vote for heading *that* way." She turned to point back the way they'd come and her face went white.

Parker followed her gaze and his blood froze. Less than three hundred yards away, a giant reptile was making its way in their direction. It had mottled brown flesh and walked on its hind legs, balancing its weight with a long tail. The monster was easily twelve feet tall at the shoulder, and it had a perpetual grin of scimitar-shaped teeth. It sniffed the ground as it walked, like a dog following a scent trail. To his horror, Parker realized it was following their footprints.

"Just out of curiosity..." Sara said.

"Yeah?"

"This dinosaur you mentioned..."

"Yeah?"

"Would it be dangerous?"

"Not terribly," Parker lied. "Still, discretion might be the better part of valor in this situa..."

Parker stopped talking when he realized he was talking to himself. Sara was already fleeing into the jungle. He ran after her, desperately trying to figure out what to do even as he tried to catch up. He had a terrible feeling they were going from the frying pan into the fire.

Behind him, Parker heard the dinosaur howl, and he glanced back to see its eyes locked on him. It was trying to chase them, but its powerful legs had trouble finding traction in the sand. It was still hundreds of yards down the beach.

Parker's feet stung from the countless sticks, stones, and—doubtless—small animals he was trampling as he ran, and the enormous webs that permeated the forest tugged on his arms and stuck in his hair. On top of that, he felt a thousand tiny scrapes all over his body from nettles, thorns, and God knew what else. At this rate, it was only a matter of time before they injured themselves. Then they'd be easy prey.

He looked back and saw the dinosaur struggling through the thick growth. Its size was a disadvantage as it attempted to catch them, and they had already expanded their lead.

"Slow down," Parker called to Sara.

Sara didn't seem to hear. She kept running full tilt, but a moment later she pitched forward and hit the ground with a "whoof!"

Parker knelt to help her up. Her legs and feet were covered with small scrapes, but none seemed bad; her slicker had protected the rest of her. "Are you hurt?" he asked, pulling her back to her feet.

Sara's eyes opened wide as she stared back over his shoulder. "Look out Parker!"

Parker turned in time to see the dinosaur's gaping jaws emerge from a thick growth of vines and creepers behind him. He pushed Sara away from the massive mouth and ducked to avoid the jaws. He heard Sara scream just as the monster's jaws snapped together inches short of Parker's head, producing a sound that almost blew out his eardrums.

Parker couldn't believe his luck. The dinosaur was hung up in some vines and couldn't quite reach him. It howled in fury and tried to work its way closer to him, but Parker didn't wait around. He turned to find Sara and saw she'd disappeared through a hole in some fern leaves.

That was when he remembered hearing her scream.

Parker poked his head through the opening and saw Sara rolling down a long, steep decline deeper into the jungle. He leapt after her. Then he was slipping and tumbling after Sara, trying hard to stabilize himself even as an endless sea of rocks and stones bit into him.

As he tumbled, Parker looked back and saw their pursuer sniffling at the top of the hill. It looked at him uncertainly, like a dog losing its favorite chew toy. Then it roared and stepped forward. An instant later, it was tumbling down the incline, as well.

Sara hit the bottom first. She rolled onto her side in a fetal position and was still. Then Parker hit. His whole body ached, but he grabbed Sara around the waist as he stood and half-carried her away as fast as he could.

The dinosaur struck the end of the decline a moment later, making the earth tremble under

Parker's feet. He looked back to see the massive animal slide through the mud and leaves at the base of the hill and into a dense patch of trees. It collided with them with a bone-crushing crunch and a rain of coconuts and palm fronds.

Parker hoped the animal had cracked its skull, but when he paused to look back he saw it was already getting back to its feet.

They couldn't keep going much longer. Parker's back was killing him and his feet were numb. It was a miracle they hadn't broken their necks, but Sara was limping. It was all they could do to maintain a hopping jog, and Sara was obviously in agony.

"I'm sorry, doll," he said. He didn't add that it would be over soon, but he was pretty sure of their fate.

Then, without warning, the jungle opened out onto a wide, grassy clearing. That would have been jarring enough, but at its center, just fifty yards ahead, was a perfectly preserved Greek temple.

"Is that real?" Sara asked between huffs.

"It sure looks real," Parker said. He'd been to the Parthenon several times, and this temple could have been its twin. At least the twin of the Parthenon when it had been built thousands of years ago. Unlike the ruins in Athens, this temple was still alabaster white with crisp carvings and rich colors.

More importantly, at least for the moment, the temple's columns were close together—they might be too narrow for the dinosaur to get through. Parker altered their direction to head for it.

He heard the monster's footfalls behind them, and then he could feel their vibration. As they reached the base of the temple's steps, he felt the dinosaur's hot breath on his shoulders. He didn't dare look back and risk breaking stride as he helped Sara up the stairs and through the columns. Only when they reached the inner walls of the temple did he chance a look back.

The dinosaur had stopped at the foot of the stairs and was shaking its head back and forth in agitation.

"What's going on?" Sara asked. "Why'd it stop?"

"I can think of a hundred reasons," Parker said. "None of them good."

Sara slumped to the floor next to the wall and looked back at the dinosaur. "Then keep them to yourself. At least it isn't eating us."

Parker kept a wary eye on the dinosaur while he checked Sara's ankle. It wasn't broken, or even badly sprained. That was a relief. Even a minor injury in their current situation would be insurmountable.

Parker decided to have a look around. He found the temple unsettling, but there weren't a lot of options. The dinosaur showed no sign of leaving, and there was no reason to think its reticence to enter the temple would last indefinitely. If it came after them, whatever help they'd have would have to come from inside their gilded cage.

Parker made a circuit of the temple's inner walls, which were uniformly blank. He could just make out the seams between the massive marble blocks that constituted the wall, but they were so finely carved he couldn't fit the tip of his knife between them. Maybe the temple was actually a tomb. If so, it was an ominous portent of their own fate.

Sara limped up from the other side of the wall. "Parker, someone's coming."

"What?" Parker almost laughed and followed her back to the front of the temple.

Sara pointed toward the far edge of the clearing. He followed the path of her finger and was astounded to see a woman walking towards them.

"She came out of the jungle," Sara said.

That would have been astonishing enough, but the woman was as anachronistic as the temple. She wore a bronze helmet in the Greek style, with a nose guard and crest down its middle; she held a javelin in her right hand and a large shield with the relief of an eagle in her left. She wore sandals and a pleated skirt but was naked from the waist up.

The dinosaur turned at the woman's approach. Parker expected it to charge her, but it began mewling and lowered its head so that its arms rested on the ground. The woman ignored the animal and approached the bottom of the temple steps. She stopped and regarded Parker and Sara coldly.

"Poi say?" The woman said.

Parker walked down the steps to meet the woman face to face. He kept an eye on the dinosaur, but it seemed rapt by the woman. When he reached the woman, he was amazed to see she would have been as tall as him even without her helmet, and her arms and shoulders were as muscular as any man's he'd ever seen. She was all woman, though, if her sun-bronzed chest was any indication. Her hair was bright blonde and she had sullen blue eyes. If not for the cruel sneer on her lips, Parker would have found her stunning.

Sara walked up beside him, though she kept a step or two back.

"Poi say?" the woman repeated. There was a cutting edge to her voice.

"Hello," Parker said. "I'm sorry, I don't understand you."

The warrior woman leveled her spear at Parker's chest, so he backed away, taking Sara's hand to pull her with him.

Something sharp jabbed him in the back. He

raised his hands and turned slowly to see that more women, each as formidable—and as naked—as the first, had appeared behind them. He hadn't heard them approach. Some carried short swords, some tridents and some spears, but Parker had no doubt they all were deadly.

"Now, take it easy, ladies. There's no need to lose your tempers."

Sara punched Parker hard in his shoulder.

"Ouch—what'd you do that, for?"

"This could only happen to you!"

At this, the first warrior—the blonde—laughed heartily. She stepped closer to Sara and gave her a cursory inspection that reminded Parker of a drill instructor looking over a raw recruit. Then she said something to the others that elicited laughter.

"What are you laughing about?" Sara asked. Parker could hear the hurt in Sara's voice.

Parker didn't blame her for being hurt. He didn't like being the butt of their jokes, either, but he was more concerned with trying to communicate with them. Their language sounded familiar. It was a lot like Greek—maybe it was a dialect—but he couldn't make out any of the words.

"What do you want with us?" Sara demanded.

The blonde woman planted her spear in the ground, then leaned her shield on it. Thus unburdened, she poked a few times at Sara's oilskin jacket. Each time, she said something to her comrades, and they responded with more laughs. Finally, the warrior woman tore Sara's jacket off, sending her sprawling to the ground.

Parker got between the warrior woman and Sara to protect her, but he could tell the women were shocked by what they'd seen in Sara, and their humor had faded to what he took to be rage.

"What is it? What's wrong?" He glanced back at

Sara, who looked bewildered.

The first warrior spat words at him with such vitriol he could feel them in his spine. Then she shoved him hard so that Parker actually staggered back until one of the other women caught him. She pushed him forward with ease. She was easily as strong as he was.

The blonde pounded on her chest. She was daring Parker to attack her.

"No," Parker said. "I won't hit a woman."

The woman kicked him hard in his stomach, making him double over. She screamed at him and pounded her chest again.

"I won't hit a woman," Parker repeated.

The woman kicked him in the face. Parker saw stars and fell onto his back. She stood over him and pounded her chest again. She was red with fury.

Parker tasted his own blood—it felt like his nose might be broken. "I c-can't hit a woman. I just can't."

"For God's sake, Parker, just punch the bitch!" Sara yelled.

Parker struggled to his feet as the other warrior women whistled and hissed at him. His knees felt like pudding, but he managed to steady himself and stand up straight. Then, making a chopping motion with his hand he said, "No!"

Whatever rationality had been in the first woman's eyes left them at that point. She howled like a wild animal and leapt onto Parker, wrapping her thighs around his neck and then falling back. Parker went over—his head caught in the leg lock. It felt like he was locked in a vise. All he could see as he tried to break her hold was the woman's behind.

At the circus there was a strong man called Ivan the Magnificent. He had once explained to Parker that muscles were like thick chords lined up under a man's skin. When that man was particularly muscular and particularly lean, you could see those chords like striations under his skin. Ivan could never seem to get that lean, although he certainly had the muscle.

Lying there—the edges of his vision going black—Parker watched as the striations started at the bottom of the warrior woman's buttocks and slowly bloomed all the way up to the base of her spine as she really laid on the pressure. A s he lost consciousness, Parker was sure that was the last thing he would ever see.

* * *

Parker heard a faint drip—drip—drip. For a moment he thought he was back in his room in Montevideo—the one with the leaky faucet and the drooping clothesline Sara had strung over the tub to dry her unmentionables. Sara!

Parker's eyes shot open and he tried to stand up but he couldn't move—he felt heavy weights across his legs, chest and arms—like iron chains. Firelight flickered on the room's ceiling, which looked like it was made of stone. Was he in a tomb? He felt dampness—wherever he was, the air was thick with moisture, oppressively so.

A face appeared over him. It was masked in shadow and he thought it was a woman's at first, with long, styled hair and smooth, fleshy cheeks. Parker thought he saw the traces of makeup on the man's face; he even smelled flowery perfume. But when the face moved back a little, he saw that it belonged to a man. The man was staring at Parker with fascination.

"Who are you?" Parker tried to look around, but it was too dark to see much beyond the strangely effete man. "Where am I?"

"Ba-ba-ba-ba," the man said in a mocking tone, opening and closing his right hand in a way that mimicked a gibbering mouth.

"Okay—I get it—you don't understand me. You don't have to be a pill about it."

"Ba-ba," the man said, again. This time a little less enthusiastically, as though he'd made his point and lost interest. He got up and started to walk away.

Parker watched as the man walked off into the shadows. Even his garments were womanly, from a plunging back on his tunic to a flowing pleated skirt. "Hey, pally," Parker called after him, "how's about turning on a light?"

Then the man was gone.

"I'd like to have a look around," Parker said to himself, completing his thought.

The sole source of light in the chamber was a flickering torch. It sputtered weakly in a corner, and illuminated just enough of the walls around it for Parker to see they were made of stone blocks like the temple walls. Maybe that meant he was inside them.

From the humidity and the dripping, he assumed there was a large pool of water in the room. He would have liked a drink of it. It was a struggle to breathe with the weight of the chains on his chest, and he was drenched in sweat.

Parker passed the time in the dark dungeon for what seemed like hours, but could have been days, fading in and out of sleep and worrying about Sara. He lost all track of time.

Until, with jarring suddenness, his solitude was broken as he heard a heavy bolt being pulled back. The stone vault—for that's what he saw it was—was flooded with light from dozens of torches, and a procession of the warrior women entered by a flight of stairs at its far end.

Each woman was more beautiful than the last, some as blonde as the first, others with the olive complexion more common on the Greek islands, and each girded with bronze armor and armed with ancient Greek weaponry. As in the jungle, they were all bare-chested and undeniably fit.

Could these women be the descendants of the legendary Amazons—straight out of Greek mythology? Had they journeyed to a South American island in the days of ancient Greece and remained there, preserving their ancient way of life?

Among their ranks, Parker saw the angry blonde who'd nearly strangled him with her iron haunches. She smiled at him with a savage fury, seeming to take delight in his helplessness. But it was another Amazon who most caught his eye. She wore a flowing purple cloak and a high crest on her helmet that marked her at once as the leader. Perhaps she was a distant descendant of Hippolyta or Penthesilea.

"You must be the woman in charge," Parker said as haughtily as two hundred pounds of iron links on his chest would allow. "If you're here to apologize, I accept."

An amused smile crossed her face. She made a sweeping gesture with both arms and the other Amazons spread out around Parker. Two grabbed him under his shoulders and lifted him to his feet effortlessly. As he rose, the chains that had been on his chest fell and nearly crushed his toes. He was able to move them out of the way at the last instant.

From his new vantage point, Parker could see the source of the moisture and the dripping sound. There was a large rectangular pool in the middle of the chamber. It was about nine feet wide and fifteen feet long, and it was covered by a massive iron grate connected to chains at both ends. Parker assumed these chains allowed the grate to be pulled back and forward when access to the pool was necessary. Or, perhaps, when access to the chamber was necessary. A brass shield hung near the pool, suspended from a rope to a wooden frame. A wooden mallet hung on the frame. Some sort of gong?

Parker put two and two together, and knew he didn't want to be chained up in that chamber when they rang that gong. As if to underscore this, the chamber walls were adorned with friezes of men on Greek triremes being pulled overboard by massive tentacles.

The queen—for that was what Parker took her to be—walked over to him. She took her time, looking him over from head to toe. Parker returned the favor. It seemed polite, and she was a real looker.

When she reached him, she took his jaw in her right hand and lifted his head so she could study his face more closely. Parker felt the restrained strength of the queen's grip. The whole time, the amused smile never left her lips. *"Api po esta?"*

It was a question, but she'd spoken so softly Parker knew she'd been addressing herself. Not that he could make heads or tails of it, anyway. So much for his education in the classics.

The queen let go of Parker and he felt the weight of his chains again. It was only then that he realized just how powerful her grip had been. What he wouldn't have given to have a dish like her in his side show.

The queen snapped her fingers and the warriors behind her parted. A woman with gray hair and olive skin stepped forward. Although much older than the others, she was still clearly a warrior despite the fact that she was unarmed and unadorned, dressed in a loincloth and sandals. The older woman stepped up until she was just behind the queen's right shoulder, and there she waited.

The queen gestured, and the woman said to Parker, *"Habla español?"*

"Si!" Parker felt relief wash over him.

The woman looked as relieved as Parker felt. "I have come[1]," she continued in broken Spanish, *"from the outskirts to speak for my queen. When I talk, it is her. When you speak, it is to her."*

Parker nodded. "Sure, you're the translator, I get it. *Si.*"

"Where are you from?"

"I'm an American," Parker said. *"I was born in Connecticut."*

The queen shook her head.

"I have never heard of Co-net-y-cut."

"It's north of here. My country is the United States," Parker said.

The queen looked annoyed.

"My queen does not believe these places are real. Why have you come here?"

"There was a storm. We fell into the water and..." Parker couldn't think of the word for "washed up." "Uh—*we floated here."*

"You and the boy-woman? Are there more of you?"

"Boy-woman? You mean Sara?"

The older Amazon looked puzzled. *"En español,"* she chided.

Parker realized he'd spoken in English. *"¡Lo siento, lo siento! I want the girl. Where is she? Is she okay? I want to see her."*

The queen guffawed and made a sweeping

---

[1] Text in italics is translated from the Spanish.

gesture before giving a command. Then Parker heard Sara cursing and shouting. A moment later she appeared at the top of the steps being pulled along by two of the Amazonian men, each as effeminate as the one Parker had seen earlier. Sara was dressed like them, and they dragged her by her hair as she pushed, pinched, and slapped at them.

They propelled her down the stairs and pushed her down at Parker's feet, hissing and spitting words at her. Then the two men hurried out of the room. The display reminded Parker of cat fights he'd seen at bars. All around him, the Amazons were laughing derisively. That was when he realized why they'd dressed Sara like one of the men—it was an insult. Their female-dominated society saw Sara in the same way Parker had seen their men. How was it possible for a society to get so mixed up?

"I have given you what you wanted. Now—are there more of you?"

Parker shook his head. "No."

"Will more come?"

Sara looked at Parker. "You know what these bimbos are saying?"

"Just this one," Parker said. "She speaks Spanish."

"Yeah?" Sara said, "Tell her they're messing with the wrong-"

"Skashay!" The queen drew her sword and in a single smooth motion had its point at Sara's neck.

Parker had been told to "shut up" in Greek enough times to recognize the word, so they *were* speaking Greek—just with an inflection that was over two-thousand years removed from the version Parker had learned.

Sara wisely kept her mouth shut.

"My queen's patience is done," the older Amazon said. *"Will more come?"*

"Not if you let us go," Parker said. *"Give us a boat and we'll leave. We won't tell anyone about you."*

The queen sneered.

"If we don't let you go, will more come?"

Parker looked the queen in her eyes. *"Ohxi."*

The Amazons gasped almost as one. He'd used the modern Greek word for "no"—something else he'd heard often enough in his travels.

The queen barked an order and the Amazons fell silent. They looked chastened as the queen sheathed her sword. She eyed Parker warily.

"You are clever like a woman, and you look strong like a woman, but we have seen your heart and you are weak. You will die. But I will give you one more chance to die like a woman."

"What do you mean I'm weak?" Parker asked.

The queen ignored Parker's question, but he saw the woman who'd bested him in the clearing smiling again. He realized he should have fought back—that he been tested and found wanting. The Amazons only respected strength. His restraint had been seen as weakness.

The queen walked to the hanging shield and used the mallet to strike it. The other Amazons in the chamber stiffened. Whatever was going to happen, it made them nervous.

"I want a rematch," Parker said.

"What's going on, Parker?" Sara asked.

"It is too late for that, now," the older Amazon said.

The water in the pool began to bubble and roil as though something large was coming up.

"Come on, Blondie, you and me! Right now, right here." He stared a challenge at the blonde Amazon, but she only laughed.

A moment later, dark green tentacles began trying to force their way through the iron grating.

They were so massive that only their tips got through—but each was as thick as one of Parker's calves. The grating—which must have weighed tons—was pushed up and scraped hard against the iron tracks in which it ran.

The Amazons began to leave the chamber until the only ones left were the two supporting Parker, the translator, the queen, and the blonde. The queen gestured to the blonde and she went to a capstan near the stairs. She gave it a slight twist and the grate pulled back a few inches.

Suddenly Parker saw a massive eye under the water. It was staring at him. Sara, who had been holding it together pretty well, all things considered, began screaming.

Parker wasn't far behind.

The queen drew her sword and dropped it at Parker's feet, then she gave a nod to the two women who'd been holding him up. He heard a click and the chains grew slack around him. Before he was free, the two women were at the top of the stairs.

The queen gave Parker a respectful nod.

"Die well."

The blonde gave the capstan another twist and the grating pulled back a few more inches.

"Wait," Parker said. He looked at the sword, at the giant eye full of green veins, and at poor, petrified Sara. *"It's true,"* he said. *"I'm not a great warrior. I'm weak—but only because I haven't been trained."*

The queen, who had turned to leave, paused at the base of the stairs.

"You are too old to be trained, now. Besides, we would never waste time training a man."

The queen turned to leave again.

"Not me," Parker said. He could hear the desperation in his voice. *"My daughters."*

The queen strode back to the edge of the grating so that the tentacles were mere inches from her feet. Behind her, the blonde Amazon's face reddened.

Parker nodded. *"That's right—look at you. If you can produce such warriors with these weak little men you have here, imagine the warriors we could make together."*

The blonde didn't seem to like what Parker was saying. She left the capstan and drew her sword, as though she wanted to gut him right then and there, but the queen glared at her and the blonde backed off.

"Spare us both, and I will give you lots of big, strong Amazon babies," Parker said.

The queen eyed Sara coldly.

"You want this one? What is she good for?"

"She will be my servant," Parker said.

The queen looked disgusted. *"A woman serving a man?"*

"She's not really a woman, is she?" Parker said, trying to use the Amazon's contempt for Sara to their advantage.

The hint of a smile crossed the queen's eyes.

"You realize what you are offering? You will be our slave—kept alive only to service us any time day or night. You will have no claim to the children you make. Yours will be a simple existence—lying with any number of us at our slightest whim. You would prefer this over the honorable death I have offered you?"

Parker looked at Sara, who had become aware something was up and had stopped screaming. He shrugged. *"It's a sacrifice I'm prepared to make."*

The queen frowned.

"I will never understand men."

* * *

Life as the Amazons' sex slave wasn't all bad. After two weeks, things had fallen into a kind of rhythm, and Parker was given most of the day to himself as the Amazons spent their time training for wars that never came, and patrolling their island on their prehistoric mounts. Apparently the Amazons had discovered the dinosaurs when they'd first come to the island, and had quickly domesticated them. They bred them as easily as they'd bred horses in ancient times.

Nights were a little less pleasant. Many of the Amazons thought Parker too "womanish" to be attractive, and a few of his visitors made him wear makeup or just look away so they didn't have to see his face. To his chagrin, the Amazon who visited him most was the blonde he'd met on his first day. Her name was Eunike. She liked to wrestle with him, and he was usually bruised in more ways than one by the time she left.

Sara, for her part, absolutely hated the situation, and she blamed Parker for causing it. She avoided him like the proverbial plague. The only time he saw her was when she attended to him in the course of her duties. Friendless and universally reviled by the Amazons, she spent most of her time holed up in her room in the small apartment they shared in the palace. He felt awful for her, and regularly swore he would find a way to get them off the island and back to civilization.

Parker spent most of his days wandering the queen's private gardens with Sofia—the older Amazon who served as his translator. She was also his guard because, as she explained it, she was too old to do much else. Sofia had not been born among the Amazons. As a young child her father had brought her with him to the island on a fishing trip.

The Amazons had killed her father, but they saw promise in Sofia—or perhaps they had just been charmed by her name, which meant "lover of wisdom" in Greek—and so they adopted her. Sofia had been allowed to train in their ways, and—when she came of age—she became one of their greatest warriors.

After Sofia, no one had come to the island again until Parker and Sara.

The first time Sofia had brought Parker to the gardens, they'd stopped at the royal library. There were manuscripts in there that would have sent Parker's archaeology buddies into apoplectic fits— particularly that guy who liked to run around with the whip. There were works by Aristotle, Sophocles, Plato, Euripides, and a bunch more Parker had never even heard of. Their words—mostly thought lost forever—had survived here, on an island paradise.

"Do you ever wonder what your life would have been like if you'd never come to this island?" Parker had asked Sofia on that day.

"I suppose I would have wound up like your friend," she said, meaning Sara. *"Small and weak as a man."*

"There are strong women where I come from," Parker said.

"Not like us."

"Not many, that's for sure. A woman like you would be famous. You would be the star attraction at my circus."

Sofia looked wistful. *"How strange your world would seem."*

That was nearly two weeks ago. On this day, Sofia had taken Parker to the royal stables to see the queen's prize mounts. They varied in skin color from deep brown to light green, and their heads were crested with spiny crowns. Each had dozens of spike-like teeth, and their mouths were twisted into perpetual grins.

"I wish I had a few of these monsters for my circus," Parker said. *"Although I'd be worried one might eat Dolly, our elephant."*

Sofia scratched one of the dinosaurs behind its ear. It was at least six feet tall at the shoulder and had a bite that could have taken Sofia's head off, yet she treated it like a pony. She looked at Parker. *"The other day, you said I would be the star of your circus. What is a circus?"*

"It's a—why it's a kind of traveling show made up of the most skilled performers and fiercest animals in the world. It goes from town to town, giving everyone a chance to see these wonders for themselves." Parker hoped he'd painted the circus in a way that would be enticing to Sofia. She was the closest thing to an ally he had on the island, and he had a sense she wasn't completely happy being a retired Amazon.

Sofia nodded. *"Do people live a long time in your world, Par-ker?"*

"Well, sure. I guess so. Sixty or seventy years. Sometimes longer. Sometimes a lot longer."

"I have seen over fifty years. Do you think my family might still be alive?"

"Sure. They couldn't be too far from here, either. Not if you came here on a fishing boat."

"I would like to see my family once before I die. The only thing I can remember is my father—the day he died."

"That's horrible," Parker said.

Sofia looked puzzled. *"He died well."*

Parker lowered his voice. *"Look, you figure out a way to get the three of us off this island, and I'll make sure you see your family again. I swear it."*

Sofia looked at Parker for a long moment, so long that he feared he'd gone too far. Then she said, *"I accept your pledge, Parker Wiley. Although I had already decided to do this. Are you sure you want to take the boy-woman woman with you? She is so...* weak."

* * *

"Good-bye, Par-ker," Eunike said. She had learned to say "hello," "goodbye", "no," and "yes" in English; and she expected Parker to be charmed by her minimal effort to speak to him in his native language. "No" was her favorite of the quartet, and Parker had heard it from her a dozen times that night. Now, as she left Parker's apartment, she pinched his bottom right where she knew she'd left a huge bruise.

"Goodbye," Parker said as he shut the door behind her. He hobbled over to the soaking bucket he kept in his chamber and sank his aching nether regions into its cool water.

As he did, Sara emerged from her own room and peered out the door after the Amazon. After a moment she shut the door. "Are you sure about this?"

"She said she'd come after my last visitor. Blondie was it. Thank God, too; I don't think I can take much more of this."

"You poor thing," Sara said without any trace of sympathy.

There was a light knock at the door. Sara cracked it open, and then opened it wider to admit Sofia.

"Are you ready?"

"Si," Parker said, slipping on the tattered remnants of his trousers. He'd worn a chiton since

he'd been put into bondage, but he wanted to leave the island as a man. "Let's make tracks."

Sofia led them through the dark corridors of the palace until they reached an ancient wooden door. It opened onto an overgrown pathway. After several minutes of crawling through the dense, bug-infested undergrowth, they came to two mounts tied to a tree.

Sara started to scream when she saw them, but Parker clamped his hand over her mouth. "S-h-h-h. It'll be okay."

"There is no way I'm getting on one of those—*things*," Sara hissed.

"You want to stay behind?"

Sara glowered at Parker. "When we get off this island, if I never see you again it'll be too soon."

"Aw, come on, doll face," Parker said, "don't be angry. Not after everything I've done for you."

Sara hauled back to slap Parker but Sofia grabbed her arm. *"What is wrong with you two? Do you* want *to be caught?"*

"Sorry," Sara said.

Parker nodded. "*Si*, me too."

Sofia released Sara's arm and Sara massaged it as Sofia crept from the bushes and checked to make sure the coast was clear. She signaled for Parker and Sara to follow her as she climbed up onto the back of the first dinosaur. Its snout swung around and Parker ducked behind the second dinosaur.

"Do not show fear," Sofia warned. *"You do not want it to see you as food."*

Parker wondered how not to look like food to a nine-foot tall meat eater as he climbed up onto its back. He reached back and took Sara's hand to help her climb on. She looked terrified but accepted his help, and soon they were racing through the jungle.

"Where are we going?" Parker asked.

"*La piscina de la luna.*"

"*¡La piscina de la luna!*" Parker said, aghast. "*En el templo. El templo donde nos encontramos?*"

"*Si.*"

Parker reined in his mount and slowed to a stop.

"What is it," Sara asked. "What's wrong?"

"She wants us to go back to that pool in the temple," Parker said. "The one with the sea monster in it."

"What?"

Sofia circled back to them. "*What is wrong? Why aren't you coming?*"

"Maybe because we don't want to die!" Parker said.

"*You will not die,*" Sofia said. "*From the moon pool it is only a short swim under the water to the lagoon. My father's ship is still there. We will use it to escape.*"

"*What about the sea monster?*" Parker asked.

"*Okay, probably you will not die,*" Sofia said.

"She's got some sense of humor," Parker said to Sara.

"*The Cephalon only comes when someone hits the golden shield. If we do not do this, we should be safe, no?*"

"No!"

Sofia looked disappointed. "*I see you are a man after all. I will take you back to the palace.*"

Sofia turned her dinosaur and started back the way they'd come.

Sara said, "Parker Wiley, I don't want to stay here another day on this wacky island. You tell her we'll do whatever it takes."

Parker sighed. He supposed being eaten by a giant sea monster was preferable to being the Amazon's sex slave, even if he couldn't see it at the moment. "Okay, okay," he called after Sofia. "*We'll do it. Let's go."*

Sofia effortlessly turned and trotted past them back on the right path. As she passed, Parker saw a smug smile on her face.

With a defeated sigh he kicked his mount into motion.

Sofia stopped them several paces away from the clearing around the temple and signaled them to keep quiet. She slipped down from her ride and vanished into the brush.

A moment later, Parker heard a subdued rustling from the trees, and Sofia reappeared, holding a spear. *"Okay,"* she whispered. *"We are on foot from here. Do not speak, and stay behind me."*

They made their way to the temple without incident, and Sofia led them up the side steps. She put down her spear and pressed hard at two unmarked points on the temple's inner wall. Suddenly the stone slid back, revealing a side door.

It was pitch dark inside, but they didn't dare risk lighting a torch. Sofia knew the way by heart, and led them by the hand down a hall to a gilded door—Parker could just make out its metallic sheen in the darkness.

There was a click as Sofia unlatched the door. They all froze and waited, listening for any sign that others were in the temple and had heard them. After a several long beats, Parker let himself breathe again. Sofia dragged the door open, and it let out a long creak as she did.

"T' simvany? E perci kapis eke?" The voice came from somewhere in the darkness behind them.

"Hurry," Sofia hissed.

Parker grabbed Sara's hand and pulled her through the door after him. It was the staircase to the vault. The familiar humidity was there, cloying at his naked chest.

He heard the door shut behind him and saw the flash of a flint. A moment later a torch flared to life on the wall and the nightmare was before him, again.

"We do not have much time," Sofia said. *"That was a priestess; she will call the guards. Help me open the grating."*

She leapt from the stairs and started turning the capstan. Parker watched her for a long second, double guessing his decision to go on this fool's errand. But there was no going back now. He hopped down and helped Sofia turn the wheel. It was incredibly heavy; he could barely budge it, and yet Sofia had been turning it on her own.

Suddenly Parker was concerned about trying to keep up with the superhuman Amazon. *"No offense, but you seem to have a really healthy set of lungs. How long will we have to hold our breath?"*

"No more than sixty heartbeats," Sofia said.

About a minute. Thank God.

There was a pounding at the top of the stairs. Someone was trying to open the door.

"I jammed it," Sofia said, *"but we do not have long. We need to be through before they get in."*

Parker looked at the pool. The grating was open enough for them to slip through. *"It'll be pitch dark—how will we know which way to swim?"*

Sofia removed her loincloth and unrolled it. She was in remarkable shape for a woman in her fifties. *"I know the way. I will swim ahead. You two will hold onto this cloth so I can guide you."*

"You're sure about the monster?" Sara asked.

"Si, no problemo. Dormido."

"It's asleep," Parker translated.

The three lowered themselves into the water and, as he took his last breath before diving, Parker saw the door to the chamber crash open. Several

Amazons charged in as he dipped under, and he hoped against hope that they hadn't seen him.

The water was ice cold, and it defied all common sense to swim into the dark abyss, but the loincloth was being pulled and he knew if he failed to keep up he'd be dead. Sofia was a powerful swimmer, and she half-dragged him through the water behind her. As they swam down he couldn't tell if Sara was still holding on. Then a faint glow appeared before them in the distance and he made out Sofia's athletic silhouette ahead. There was Sara's, too. She was just ahead of him, swimming as hard as she could.

* * *

The queen saw two of her guards dive into the moon pool as she entered the chamber. "What's going on?" she demanded.

"It's the man," one of the guards said. She didn't have to say which man. There was only one that mattered.

"Close the grating," the queen ordered as she descended the stairs to the shield. Several of the Amazons ran to obey as the queen pulled the mallet from the wooden frame. She struck the shield without a thought for the Amazons who had dived in after Parker. It would be their honor to die for their queen.

* * *

The water grew lighter. Whatever the light had been that he'd seen earlier, they were moving towards it.

Parker's lungs burned. Sofia had said no more than sixty heartbeats, but it seemed like they'd been under a lot longer. Maybe her heart beat a lot slower than his. If he was struggling, what was Sara going through?

They had swum through a short passage and were in a massive cavern. Stalactites hung from the ceiling, which funneled upwards towards an oval of darkness. Was it the surface? He hoped it was.

Sofia glanced back at him. She was making the swim effortlessly. Sara, on the other hand, was starting to look desperate. She was holding onto the cloth with her left hand, and holding her mouth closed with her right. At least she was still kicking.

Sofia made a tilting motion with her head and Parker realized she wanted him to look behind them. He did, and was dismayed to see two Amazons swimming after them. They had stripped down to their chitoniskos for buoyancy, but each still had a weapon. One had a spear, and the other a trident, and they were gaining on him.

Parker took one last look at the black surface. It was only moments away, but they'd never make it. He let go of the cloth and turned back towards the Amazons. Maybe he could slow them down enough to give Sofia and Sara a fighting chance.

The Amazon with the spear changed her course to intercept Parker, while the other continued after Sofia and Sara. He tried to swim after her, but had to dodge as the first Amazon's spear flashed out at him.

He was too slow under water, and the spear sliced through his shoulder. It wasn't deep but it hurt like hell. The Amazon jabbed again, and this time Parker was able to catch the spear and hold onto it.

He recognized the Amazon as one of the ones who'd asked him not to look at her during a visit. She rounded on him with a look of hatred, but her eyes suddenly opened wide and she gasped, letting a stream of bubbles escape her mouth. She let go of her spear and began struggling for the surface.

Parker turned in time to see a massive cephalopod flash past him, its tentacles reaching out for the Amazon. It was glowing, and—Parker realized—was the source of the ethereal light filling the cavern.

Still holding the Amazon's spear, Parker kicked toward the surface, hoping the sea monster would be too busy chasing her to see him. He watched in horror as the octopus's powerful tentacles closed around the Amazon. To her credit, she was still punching and kicking when the creature finally pulled her in to its beak.

Parker couldn't watch any more. Not that he had time. His vision began to swirl as he used up the last of his breath. He broke the surface just in time, and fresh air had never tasted so good. Parker bobbed there for several long moments, drinking it in.

"Parker!" It was Sara's voice. He turned and saw her at the water's edge. She waved for him to swim to her. "Hurry—Sofia needs your help."

Parker saw the dark-skinned Sofia—still naked and soaking wet—fighting with the trident-wielding Amazon on the beach. He swam for them as fast as he could, but just as he reached the shallows he felt something unimaginably powerful wrap around his ankle, and then he was back under.

Parker turned to see the giant cephalopod stretching its other tentacles toward him, and he thought back to his days on the Stanford football club. A good offense is the best defense. He leveled the spear at the monster's eye and charged.

By nature, cephalopods are timid creatures, and this one was, too, despite its enormous size. Seeing Parker swimming towards it, the creature suddenly changed direction and released his ankle. Parker swam after it, aiming the tip of the spear at the animal's massive eye.

Suddenly the creature seemed to remember its huge size advantage, and it moved towards Parker again. That's when the spear tip connected. The monster's eye deformed nearly a foot before the tip of the spear broke through the lens, and Parker swam on—driving the spear deeper into the creature's flesh.

It twisted away from Parker, ripping the spear from his hand, and bolted off into the distance. The creature's glow faded and left Parker in utter darkness.

By the time he got back to the surface, Parker was exhausted. He dog-paddled to the shallows and crawled up to the beach.

"Sara?"

To his relief, Sofia and Sara both emerged from the brush. Sara almost looked glad to see him. "Well, you took your time," she said. "We're trying to escape, here—remember?"

"What happened to the other Amazon?"

"Sofia took care of her," Sara said.

Sofia gestured for him to follow her into the brush. *"Help us get my father's boat into the water."*

There was a modest wooden fishing boat there. *"This looks like it's in pretty good shape,"* Parker said.

"I have taken care of it. It is all I have left of my father. No one else knows about it. We need to get it into the water, there will be more guards."

As if to underscore Sofia's warning, Parker heard shouting from the jungle. He put his shoulder into the boat's stern, and Sofia used a long branch as a lever to help move the boat into the water.

No sooner had they clambered into it then a

squad of Amazons ran out of the jungle. Parker and Sofia took up oars and began rowing with all their strength.

A few of the Amazons hurled their spears at the launch, but only one hit the boat—burying itself into the deck inches from Parker's foot. The rest fell short or went wide of the mark. The Amazons seemed afraid to venture into the water, perhaps not wanting to swim with the Cephalon, but then one of the Amazons dove into the lagoon and began swimming after them.

Parker realized it was Eunike, and he quickly sat down and got another set of oars into the water. It was no good, though. As fast as he and Sofia rowed, Eunike was gaining on them. The boat wasn't built for speed.

Sofia set her oars and stood up, but Parker said, *"No. This one's mine."*

As Eunike reached the boat and tried to board it, Parker looked down at her. She grinned at him. "Hel-lo, Par-ker."

Parker gestured for Eunike to climb into the boat, and then he put his dukes up. "I owe you this one, Blondie."

Eunike, seeing he meant to fight her, grinned savagely and began to pull herself out of the water. Before she could, Sara smacked her over the head with one of the oars. The paddle cracked from the force, and Eunike fell back into the water, too dazed to do more than stare in wonder as the trio made their escape.

* * *

Less than a day later, they were rescued by the *Periquito*. The tramp steamer had suffered storm damage, and had returned to Montevideo for repairs.

Sofia joined Parker's circus and became his greatest attraction, amazing sold out audiences with her exotic beauty and incredible prowess. True to his word, Parker tracked down Sofia's family in a Uruguayan fishing village. He took her to meet them in 1939.

But that's another story...

What's out there? Are you sure you want to find out?

HOWL

By T. L. Emery

David heard the howling just as he was drifting off to sleep. He thought he'd dreamt it. Then he heard it again; a long baying from out in the woods. It may have happened the night before, and there was a vague memory of the noise. But last night the window had been closed. Tonight it was much warmer.

While he listened, David thought back to the last time he heard the howls. It was just about this time last month, a couple days after he and Jim Knight had camped out to celebrate Jim's fifteenth birthday. He remembered the relief—as the howls filled that night—that he was safe in his room and not in a tent in the yard. He wasn't dumb; he could count, and it was almost exactly four weeks ago. But he also wasn't an idiot and the idea that came to his mind was simply ridiculous.

He looked through the screen window over the moon-bright lawn, trying to see anything in the forest beyond. There was no movement and no sounds for the moment. Then a quick bark and another howl. It had to be a dog, but it was a big one. David sat on the edge of the bed staring through the window, waiting for any motion, any noise. He strained his hearing, picturing a cartoon old-timer with a cone sticking out of his ear.

He was ready to lie back down when he heard a rustle at the edge of the yard. A twig snapped.

Closer now. David backed away from the window, not wanting it to look up and see him. His heartbeat quickened and he tried to hold his gasping breath. There it was. Something moved close to the moonlit grass. He backed away from the window as far as he could while still being able to see.

A raccoon shuffled out of the trees, and David released the lungful of air, feeling foolish.

The raccoon waddled across the yard and David stuck his face back up against the screen to watch. The howl came again, followed by a bark, and another howl. The coon spun toward the sound, then turned and scurried for the woods on the right side of the house. The howls sounded closer now. He heard a second howl from off to his left. The first voice answered with a growl, and the sounds merged together somewhere in the dark woods in a crescendo of canine vocalizations.

David slammed the window shut, threw himself under the covers and curled into a ball, hoping to sleep, but resigned to the fact that he probably wouldn't.

* * *

David awoke some hours later, sweltering in the windless room. He lifted the window and gazed at the cloudy sky and darkened yard as the dewy air blew over his face. The world was quiet except for insects and the distant hoot of an owl.

Parched, he crossed the hall to the bathroom in darkness. He felt for the sink, bent down and drank from the faucet. The hallway floor creaked. He shot up, smacking his temple on the tap. He rubbed the spot, hoping it wasn't bleeding, and then wiped his mouth with the back of his hand. An inventory sped through his mind. Mom and Dad slept downstairs, so it had to be his older sister Janice. *Yeah, Janice,* he thought, *not some howling beast that could open doors.*

He jerked the door open and saw a hand reaching for where the knob had been. Janice leapt back. "Jesus Christ, David. What's wrong with you?" She stood there, still dressed in shorts and a half shirt, holding her robe.

"Are you just getting in?" he asked.

"Mind your own business and go to bed."

There was light coming from her bedroom and he could see that her hair was a mess; not the Miss Perfect tresses that he was used to. "Were you out with that new boy?"

"Get out and go to bed," she said.

"Does Mom know?"

"No, and she's not going to either. Now get out." Janice backed up a step to let David by, and he looked down, avoiding her glare. Her feet were filthy.

"Were you out in the . . . the outside? Didn't you hear—?"

"David, get out of here and stop asking me questions, or so help me," she snarled.

He opened his mouth, wanting to ask how they could have been outside all night with those dogs howling in the woods. The room was getting brighter, clouds breaking outside. The light allowed him to see her more clearly. A leaf stuck in her hair. And there were three long scratches down her side, ending close to her hip. He stared.

Her body came closer. He didn't notice her movement, so wrapped up in looking at those scratches. He stepped back and his legs hit the toilet, arms flailing to keep his balance. David looked up at his sister. She glared, eyes full of hate.

"Never a word to anyone, you little shit. Do you hear me?"

David nodded, mouth agape, dry lips sticking to his teeth. He struggled not to ask or say something stupid.

He lost the struggle. "Mom'll be pissed."

"She'll never know." His sister's eyes scanned him and he pulled his upper body back further. "And if she does find out, I'll kill you." Janice jerked her head forward, nose twitching, and sniffed all round his face. "It might take me a month. But I'll kill you."

Turn your thermostat up, because this tale from Alan Amrhine is about strange happenings on . . .

THE COLDEST DAY

By Alan Amrhine

As I set about my evening ablutions that frigid night in January, that day others would later remark was the coldest any of them could remember, even Amos of the hollow, who was nigh on ninety-three years old; as I went about those tasks that mostly involved water, the splashing or gulping or sprinkling of water, water that was close to ice on this night in spite of the strained emanations of the potbelly stove in the parlor—I saw the angel, standing quietly, watching me.

It looked like hell.

Its wings were crumpled and seemed to be molting, as close as I could tell. It stared at me from several feet away, pulsing in a slow, rhythmic fashion, alternately fading to a white haze and then solidifying to a more substantial form. It appeared cold, as I was, which puzzled me in a disconcerting sort of way. Its skin appeared rough in spots, or maybe it was frost. I could not discern the emotion on its face—it seemed like something between boredom and fatigue.

"This all the heat you have," said the angel.

"Why, yes, I'm sorry to say," I replied in a steady and sure voice, which was remarkable since I had never conversed with an angel before and—truth be told—it seemed a strange thing for an angel to say, in any case. I was quite pleased with myself for maintaining my composure, as well as quite incredulous. "The stove puts out what it can," I added.

The angel nodded with what appeared as resignation in its eyes. "Yes," it said slowly. "I suppose we all . . ." and here it paused for the barest moment, ". . . do what we can," the angel finished, more softly than it had begun.

I blotted a towel against my dripping face and realized just how cold it had become, now that my senses were returning. Nevertheless, I was slow, methodical—taking time dabbing my forehead and around my eyes—hoping that, when I pulled the towel away, the apparition would be gone.

"No such luck."

A shiver ran down my spine. I lowered the towel from my face. "I beg your pardon?"

"No such luck," the angel repeated. "I'm still here. You were probably hoping I'd be gone. I've seen it countless times—it's a common response."

I took a deep breath. "Are you the Angel of Death?" I said boldly, sounding—at least to my ears—much more in control of the situation than I felt.

The angel laughed a slow, tired laugh, lowered its head, waggled it side to side. After a moment, it lifted its fathomless eyes to meet mine. "No, I am not. I am not the Angel of Death—although, in all honesty, I can understand there being some confusion as of late."

"I don't understand—"

The angel raised its hand. "I've just been a little off my game lately, a tad tired, a mite weary of working at this for ages." The angel wiped a hand across its face. The frost or roughened angel skin formed a white puff in the air. "I am not the angel you mentioned, Mr. Bannister. To the contrary, I am your guardian angel."

"Why are you here? Why do you appear to me on this particular night? Why now? What is going to happen?"

The angel glanced at me with those infinitely deep, infinitely sad eyes, and then looked down. "I don't know."

I stared at the angel. "What do you mean, you don't know?" I threw the towel I had been holding onto the sink stand. The violence of my action surprised me, even though anger had recently replaced grief as my dominant emotion since Martha's passing three months back. "How can you not know? Isn't that your job?"

"We're not perfect."

I turned and leaned back against the wash stand. I stared at the angel, feeling quite befuddled.

"Angels are not without fault, Mr. Bannister. We are creatures, God's creations, like yourself, albeit we walk in different realms at times and have different abilities. There is only One who is perfect."

Bile surged in my chest. "One, if that!" I shouted. I regretted my blasphemy as soon as it was out.

The angel cringed at my words, but said nothing.

"Why was an angel sent to me, obviously not a godly man at present, if ever I was? What cruel mind would will that I receive a guardian angel, when my dear Martha had none when she was hit and dragged mercilessly by a careening carriage as she stepped from the dry goods store?" My eyes burned into my hands that were now balled into fists.

The angel was silent.

After a spell, I looked up.

The angel flickered, faded, returned in a

somewhat different posture, seemingly dimmer than before. "Your wife had a guardian angel, Mr. Bannister," the angel said. "Everyone does."

"She had an angel?" I roared at the absurdity. I steadied myself with my hand against the wall, swallowed. "What kind of protector would allow a beautiful woman in the prime of life to be killed in such a senseless manner?" I closed my eyes, felt my whole body shake. Blood rushed in my brain like breaking ocean waves, pounding in my ears. After a moment, I heard a rustling of wings.

The angel cleared its throat.

I opened my eyes.

The angel's face was drawn, its shoulders and wings hunched even more. "I was your wife's guardian angel, as well, Mr. Bannister."

I felt my jaw drop; I could form no words. I fell back against the wash stand, slid down to a seated position on the cold planked floor. I heard my shaving mirror hit the floor and shatter behind me.

"I beg your forgiveness. She was not supposed to die at that time."

"Forgive you," I heard myself rasp. "Forgive you?" My breath formed clouds in the air before me. The stove would need to be stoked soon. My mind groped at that thought, not yet ready to grasp the other. *She was not supposed to die at that time. She was not supposed to die at that time? What in God's name . . .*

Still seated on the floor, I felt myself falling to the left. I stuck out my arm to catch myself, felt the broken glass against my palm. Curiously, there was no pain. I picked up a shard of glass and absently turned it between thumb and forefinger. Bulbs of red blossomed on my fingertip and dropped to the floor in an unhurried succession. I felt nothing.

"I am old," the angel said. "Old and weary and

not particularly gifted. I never was."

"You are a goddamned *angel*," I said weakly. My numbness was beginning to fade.

"And you are a human being. You are of the same essence as every other human being on this Earth, and yet you are not exactly like any of the others. You have different talents; you have different amounts of will; you have different amounts of heart. Some humans are great leaders. Others live quiet and sedate lives, barely causing a ripple. Some are courageous and self-sacrificing; others cower and maim and rob. Some are innovative and prosper, others sweep out stables and struggle to live. It is not much different with angels. We angels are not all like Michael the Archangel; you humans are not all like President Lincoln.

"And what sort are you?" I said, rage once again stoked within me. I spat the words: "Are you the angelic equivalent of a saloon sot, sleeping drunk and foul in the gutter? *You let my wife die!*"

The angel was silent. It hung its head.

"And where is God in this? A very poor manager of inept guardian angels, is he? He wants us to pray to him, to bow to him, to give him obeisance—and this is what we get? A broken down has-been of an angel—a never-was by his own admission—whose job it was to protect my Martha and who . . ." I was shouting, railing now, and I could not control it. *"It's no damnable wonder I was forced to call on the devil!"*

The wind picked up outside, whistling sleeves of cold through the cracks around the lavatory window, reaching fingers of ice and rustling the curtains Martha had stitched just last summer.

The angel's head jerked up. Its eyes were wide. It stared at me with an intensity previously not exhibited; stared at me with something akin to trepidation. "You have sought out Lucifer?"

I felt foolish now, even amidst the anger I felt for this pathetic angel and his God. I hadn't meant to blurt that out; indeed, it was merely a passing thought, a cry of desperation into an empty void the night previous—a futile plea for the return of my wife which I knew was not possible, but neither was it possible to continue living without her.

"When did this happen? What did you do? Has he sealed your soul yet?"

"*Nothing* happened," I said. Why did I feel the need to explain? Explain I did, nonetheless. "It was nothing—a careless remark brought about by insufferable loneliness and grief. In a moment of deepest despair I cried that I would make a deal with the devil himself if only I could have my Martha back."

"When?" The angel's voice had an urgent quality.

"Last evening, about this time . . . maybe a little later. What does it matter?" My anger was circling, ready to come roiling back like a ball on a tether.

"He will come here tonight, Mr. Bannister. Lucifer always comes in person to seal the deal, and always twenty-four hours from when the words are first spoken. He will be here for your signature, so to speak." The angel flickered.

"Lucifer is real? I always thought him a myth, a bugaboo to explain away God's mistakes."

"You didn't believe in guardian angels until tonight."

"I *still* don't." I felt my lip curl into a sneer. "At least, I don't believe in any guardian angel who's worth a damn." I exhaled harshly. "Or your absentee God who countenances inept help." I reached into the open closet, withdrew a coarse woolen blanket, and draped it over my shoulders. The heaviness of the blanket seemed to weigh on my spirit as well as my shoulders. "I'm not in the habit of being rude, but I'm going downstairs to tend the stove and eventually get some sleep near the source of what little heat there is. You can go wherever you like. I don't need you."

"You would not fare well facing Lucifer alone," the angel said.

"I'd be better off with you there?" I shook my head. "I would laugh in your face if I could find any humor here whatsoever. As it is, my melancholy is upon me once again. Just leave me be, if there's any decency in you at all."

I descended the stairs from the loft to the main room of the cabin, and saw the stove was barely glowing. I opened the door, stirred the ashes, and tossed in some new splits of seasoned hickory. Closing the door brought a muted clang of hot iron, and I retired to my chair and pulled the blanket tighter. A slow-burning kerosene lamp on a table by the door, and the vents in the potbelly stove door, provided the only light. Shadows danced on shadows—lighter gray over dark, darker gray over black—but it was all the light I needed anymore. Darker than this was my soul.

I must have started to doze, all curled up in one of the two stuffed chairs in the sparsely furnished room, when suddenly my eyes sprang wide. The angel was but two feet from my chair, looking at me straightaway.

"What were your words last night?" the angel asked.

"I told you. Now leave me—"

"Again—what exactly did you say?"

I was morose and tired, and enraged once again by this meddlesome and incompetent angel. I verily shouted at him. "I said, 'I would make a deal with the devil himself if I could have my Martha back!' "

The angel's eyes bore into mine. "And what would you give in such a deal? You have no wealth or property."

"My soul, you ignoramus," I screamed. "What does anyone give in these circumstances? I would give my soul!"

At once the room blazed with light as I feebly tried to shield my eyes. The angel was now tall and straight, burning bright as the sun, its wings full and flexing—in truth, beautiful and majestic. Its hand flashed once, twice across my forehead. "It's been a pleasure dealing with you, Mr. Bannister." It waved its arm to the right in a sweeping gesture. "And now, our business is concluded."

At once I went blind, or at least it seemed so. Gradually, ever so gradually, the stove slits and lamp became dim cotton balls in the darkness, until finally they took shape and I could see dimly, as before. I blotted my hand against my burning forehead and, when I pulled it away, the lines of blood left on my palm formed a strange and disturbing pattern.

As I looked across the room, in the dim light of the lantern I saw Martha slumped in the other stuffed chair, looking more like strewn clothes. Her right arm dangled over the side, her fingers almost touching the floor. In a voice like the scraping of ancient cave stones, she said, "Is this all the heat you got?" Then her jaw dropped, made a sickening snap, and then dropped impossibly more. There was then a high-pitched keening sound that seemed to go on and on, which even now I'm unsure as to whether it emanated from her or me.

When the Constable came to our home in the morning to break the news that my wife's grave had been robbed, he seemed quite unnerved when first beholding Martha. Constable Ben's face twisted through a full range of emotions as I told him the story of Guardian Angel Lucifer and the events of the evening past. Martha, stubborn as I had forgotten she could sometimes be, stayed quiet the whole time and would not corroborate my story in the least.

When they put me on trial—I suppose for making a deal with the devil, as Rutherford Glen is in a very staid Christian county—I remember there was dissension and disagreement in the gallery. Ned Sanders kept asking as to how anyone could have shoveled through that cold, hard earth this time of year, especially with all the rains that had packed that graveyard clay back in November. Martha didn't attend any of the proceedings, which concerned me at first until I reasoned she must be keeping the home fires burning, tending to matters in my absence.

Yes, it seemed like everybody present had a different opinion of this or that—it was hard to follow it all. One thing they did all agree on, however, was the statement old Amos of the hollow had proffered early on: "It was the coldest day anyone could remember."

For a respite from all the gloom, here's a Christmas story, though – okay – some of it's on the gloomy side, as well. It takes place on the Great Plains, in the early 1880s.

THE MIRACLE

By Robert Broomall

The next day was Christmas. It was too cold to blow reveille, so Clatterbuck, the trumpeter, went round the tents, shouting the men awake. The Swede poked his head out of the tent he shared with Irish Tom.

"Santa bring us anything?" Tom asked.

"A foot of snow," Swede said.

"Grand fellow, Santa. Just what we needed."

Swede looked at the next tent, where their messmate Nails Morrison was using his tin mess cup to shovel snow away from his shelter's entrance. "Smitty still alive?" Swede asked.

Nails made a sour face. "Don't see me buryin' him, do you?"

Around them in the gray light, the rest of C Company crawled out of their half-buried tents. The wind had fallen. The day dawned crystal clear, the snow a white blanket stretching to the horizon. There were saw-toothed mountains in the distance. The Tetons, somebody said.

Roll was taken. No one had frozen to death during the night, and there were still just the three cases of frostbite, though one of the victims, "Big" Abner Small, looked likely to lose some of his toes. With the other two men, it was uncertain. In honor of the day, the Captain halted the march and let the company remain in camp. C Company's thirty-odd men greeted the news quietly. They were too cold and footsore to do more. The Captain had Bible Bob read the Gospel according to Saint Luke. Normally the men didn't care much about religion, but on this day they listened attentively to the story of Jesus' birth. A light guard was set. The Captain sent details to hunt and gather firewood, and the rest of the men were dismissed.

* * *

A few of the boys crawled back into their canvas tents and tried to sleep; the rest gathered around their mess fires and prepared breakfast. They moved slowly and a bit awkwardly. Most wore three layers of clothing—all that they owned—under their light blue overcoats, with newspapers stuffed between the layers. Their feet and lower legs were wrapped with strips of buffalo skin, hairy side out, and they wore ungainly mittens of the same material, fashioned for them by the ladies at the fort. Some wore wool sailor's caps, pulled low over their ears; others had thick scarves tied over their campaign hats and beneath their chins. And even though most wore bandannas or scarves across their faces so that only their eyes showed, their beards were frozen stiff; ice rimed their mustaches and the hair beneath their lips.

"Look at all this snow," said the Swede, beating his arms against his sides. "Think we'll be able to pick up the Sioux trail?"

"I hope not," said Irish Tom. "Then we can go back to the fort." Tom was a compact, energetic young man with black hair and prominent teeth. He had come by his nickname to distinguish him from "Long Tom" Wilkens, who had since taken his discharge.

"We ain't goin' back," growled the First Sergeant, coming up behind them. "Fitzpatrick could track a fly through the Sahara."

The men moaned. The company been called out on a ten-day scout that was supposed to have gotten them back to the fort on the 23d. But they'd come across cattle that looked to have been butchered by a party of Sioux—no doubt off the reservation because they were starving—and they'd taken up the "hostiles'" trail.

Ogle, the recruit, said, "But with us stoppin' for the day, how are we goin' to catch them Injuns?"

"Cap'n don't want to catch 'em," the First Sergeant said. "He just wants to get 'em back on the reservation without nobody gettin' killed."

"Why do we have to do this, anyway?" Ogle went on. "Ain't chasin' Injuns a job for the cavalry?"

"Cavalry." The First Sergeant gave a derisive laugh. "This is work for real sojers—infantry work." The First Sergeant was the only man in the company, besides the captain, who had fought in the war, and that made him, in the eyes of the men, very old. Normally he would only speak to a recruit like Ogle to damn his eyes or order him on some punishment detail, but this was Christmas. "Yellow legs is useless at all times, but 'specially in winter. It's too hard gettin' 'em grain for their horses. Now, us, we can march forever. They ain't got to feed us grain. They ain't got to feed us nothin'. We can live off snow and shoe leather, if we have to."

"Pretty much what we *are* livin' off of," cracked Irish Tom.

* * *

Each man in Private Smith's group of four had

his job at mess. Nails' job was making coffee. He roasted the men's green coffee beans in a small frying pan. When they were done, he smashed them with the butt end of his bowie knife and put them in boiling water to steep. While they were steeping, he thought about tonight. He'd figured the company might be out over Christmas, so he'd hidden a pint of brandy in his pack, and tonight, when he had guard, he was going to drink it. Barracks etiquette demanded that he share with his bunky, and strongly suggested that he include his other two mess mates, as well, but Nails didn't care. He was going to drink it by himself.

The sun was rising as Swede and Irish Tom helped Smith out of his tent and sat him by the cook fire, wrapped in his gray blanket. Private John Smith, called "Johnny Five Aces" or "Bottom of the Deck Johnny" by the other men in the company, was Nails's bunky. Bunkies shared tents, they shared blankets, they shared everything. It was Nails's job to take care of Smith. "Coffee?" Nails asked him. He snapped off the word, more like an accusation than a question.

Smith nodded. He'd come down with a fever right after the march began. The fever had turned to pneumonia, and the combination of snow and sub-freezing temperatures had worsened his condition steadily. Beneath his filthy beard, his skin was sallow. His eyes were sunken, with dark circles under them. His breathing seemed to have become more labored just since reveille.

"Think he'll last the day?" Swede asked.

Nails held a tin cup to Smith's mouth. "I hope not."

"Jaysus," said Tom, as he dished out their breakfast. "There's a fine Christian sentiment."

Smith's feverish eyes returned Nails's glare. The

two men had fought a number of times; Smith had once beaten Nails senseless with his belt buckle. Nails wasn't the type to back down, though. The day he'd gotten out of the hospital, he'd fought Smith again. Nails had asked for a new bunky, but the First Sergeant declined—no one else wanted to be with Smith.

"Why should I pretend?" Nails snarled. "We're well rid of this bastard. When he ain't in the guardhouse, he's drinking or fighting or cheating us at cards. I'll bet anything he's the one that's been stealing from the barracks."

"I know," said Tom, "but on Christmas? No wonder they call you a hard case." The hardest case in the company, they said. No one liked him.

Nails jammed some food, a mush of hardtack and salt pork, into Smitty's mouth. "Screw Christmas. It's just another day. There's nothing special about it, nothing magic. There's no miracles, like in that Dickens story."

"That's where you're wrong," said Tom. "If ever there's a day for miracles, 'tis Christmas."

"I'd like to see one out here."

"You may, lad. You just may."

* * *

After breakfast, some of the boys tried to have a snowball fight, but the snow was too dry to make snowballs. The Lieutenant, whom the men called the Athlete, tried to organize footraces or a tug or war, but no one was interested. The firewood details returned. The Captain let the men build a bonfire to go with their mess fires. Corporal Hinkle—called Horsethief in deference to his civilian occupation— and some of the boys asked the Captain if they might be permitted to cut a tree. He waved them to it, and they got a couple axes from the pack mule and started toward the distant hills, their whoops echoing across the frozen plains. The rest of the men returned to their mess fires, which had become their temporary homes.

* * *

It was funny how quick you settled in, Nails thought. Men lounged in the snow beside the fires like they'd been there all their lives—comfortable, like they were settling into a favorite chair back home. Other men wandered back and forth between the fires, visiting. A few games of cards started. More coffee was made.

It was Swede's turn to bathe Smith's red-hot forehead and face with snow. "What do you think they're doing back at the fort?" he said to the others. "Do you think they've started the jollification?"

" 'Tis entirely certain they have," said Irish Tom. "Living the high life, they are. And us stuck out here."

"Christmas ain't about feasts," said Bible Bob from the next fire. "It's about the Baby Jesus."

Nails made a deprecating noise. The Swede was thoughtful. He had a big, open face, like a cherub's, framed by blond hair. "It's more than that," he said. "Christmas is about home, and family."

"What a bunch of crap," Nails said. " 'Home?' 'Family?' What's that to somebody like me? I grew up in an orphanage."

"Did you never know your parents at all?" asked Big Abner Small. The burning pain in Abner's frostbitten feet had turned to numbness, and he thought that meant he was going to be all right.

Nails shook his head. "Heard they died of cholera. Don't know if it's true."

"Brothers? Sisters?" said Big Abner.

Nails shrugged. "I used to wonder about that. Don't, any more."

When he was done with Smith, Swede swirled a fresh cup of coffee in his tin cup. He held his face over the cup, letting the hot fumes drift up and thaw his nostrils. He took on a dreamy, far-away look. "I sure wish I was home," he said. "Back home on Christmas, we'd pile into the wagon and go to my uncle's farm —he's got the biggest house in the family. We'd get there on Christmas Eve, and we'd be so excited we couldn't sleep. First thing next morning, there'd be the smell of Grandma's butter pound cakes cooking. We'd go to church, come back and get our presents, then sit down to a gut-buster of turkey and dressing and more cakes and pies than you can shake a stick at. After, there'd be dancing for the growed-ups and older kids, and the younger ones would play with their new toys and try not to get in too much trouble."

Irish Tom stuffed tobacco in his clay pipe and lit it. "What I remember about Christmas is me Ma's mince pie, with rum sauce. Waited all year for that mince pie, we did. Poor Ma, she's gone now." He crossed himself, and his eyes softened. "We didn't have much in the way of presents, but there was always a special feeling on Christmas Day. So maybe Christmas is about memories, as well."

"Never had a Christmas I wanted to remember," said Nails.

"Not one? That's hard to believe."

"Is it? Let's see . . . " Nails jabbed the fire with his bayonet, producing a shower of red sparks. "You got a sweet roll if you were lucky. Maybe a second serving of gruel. Course, the matrons took off that day, so the bigger kids could whomp on you all day without nobody to stop them. That was Christmas at the orphanage. A hell of a time. Great memories."

"You got no presents?"

"A shirt, maybe, or pair of pants, made at the workhouse, which is where we were headed when we came of an age. Well, no thank you very much, says I. I skipped out of there and I never looked back."

* * *

Beside them, Smith sat huddled over, shivering with fever, wrapped in his blankets. His mess mates' words drifted in and out of his consciousness. Christmas. Christmas last year had been debauchery at a Lexington whore house. He didn't remember much of it, even the part that was responsible for him being here now. The year before, it had been the same thing, only in another town. He and the men he associated with had no families. They lived in shanties, by themselves or with whores. They spent their time in saloons—drinking, gambling, fighting among themselves. What was Christmas to them?

And yet . . .

Memories, unbidden, floated up from the depths of Smith's feverish brain. Voices, long forgotten, spoke once more . . .

His mother's musical lilt: "If you eat all the dough, there won't be any for the cookies . . . "

His father's baritone: "Here you are, son. All the way from New York . . . "

And his sister, laughing, teasing: "Do it the other way, silly . . . "

Smith stirred. Where had these visions come from? Here came his father, young and strong, carrying in the tree before a roaring fire. There was his mother, setting the cloth on the table, humming Christmas songs; and himself and his sister making decorations from colored paper, painted nuts and bits of tin foil from the inside wrappings of plug tobacco. Threading the tree with stings of berries and popcorn after Father had carefully put on the candles.

"Don't burn the house down," Father always told them.

"We won't," he and his sister would say, and of course there was always one near accident that had their mother in panic and left himself and his sister rolling on the floor in laughter at the telling of it afterward.

His sister. He hadn't thought of her in years. He wondered where she was now. Married, likely, with children of her own, if she hadn't died in childbirth or been carried off by disease. They'd lived a ways from the other families, so he and his sister had been thrown together.

They'd slept in the same bed when they were little, giggling and talking through the night till Pa came and made them be quiet. They'd shared everything—hopes, fears. They were playmates, friends, fellow explorers and defiers of nature. They'd gone swimming together, and hunting. Because of him, she could shoot as good as most boys. Because of her, he'd developed an interest in books . . .

* * *

Horsethief Hinkle and the boys returned, carrying an eight-foot spruce tree. They set up the tree in the snow, near the bonfire. Having set it up, they had to decorate it. That stumped everybody, till Ben the Walrus took off his brass belt buckle and attached it to one of the tree's branches. Each man in the company followed suit, including the Captain, and, lastly, the Athlete, till the tree had thirty-odd belt buckles hanging from its branches. Welsh Willie affixed his bayonet by its socket to the tree top, and if you squinted you could pretend it was a star . . .

* * *

Smith remembered other Christmases, after Father had left for the war and never returned. He remembered his stepfather's shouts, his sister's screaming at him to stop, his mother sobbing while his stepfather took away his books—and when Smith had tried to get them back, the bastard had slapped him across the room.

"Don't hold with books," he'd said. "Reading's for lazy folk. Only one book worth a damn, and that's the Good Book. Rest is useless, you ask'n me,"

After his stepfather came, there was no more skylarking in the woods, no more reading Waverly *or* Fenimore Cooper *under the old shade tree on a hot day. It was work, from dawn till dusk and then some. For him and his sister. No more school. Clearing land—chopping wood and hauling logs, wrestling with the mule, plowing and planting until his hands bled, and it was never good enough. There was always more to do..*

When he was fifteen, Smith could take no more. He ran away. He'd drifted down to a river town, hoping to find work. On the way, he'd been robbed of what little he had, beaten and left in a heap by the road. He hadn't quit, though. He'd gone to work for a blacksmith but found he had the wanderlust—maybe the books had done that to him. He never stayed in one spot for long, and before too much time had passed, necessity had forced him into a life of crime—robbery and assault. Along with these had come drink and cards and women, and soon his old life had been forgotten in the immediacy of the new and the need to stay alive from one day to the next.

There had been one moment when he might have changed. There had been a girl—blonde ringlets and eyes like cornsilk. She reminded Smith of his sister. There had been a Christmas with her. He'd even gone to church, dressed up in a store-bought suit. But her parents hadn't approved of him, and he wouldn't abandon his companions, and eventually she drifted away, to a man who could give her peace and security . . .

* * *

"What happened after you left the orphanage?" Swede asked Nails.

Nails had removed his right shoe, then peeled the three socks from his foot. The three socks made the damn shoe too tight, and not only did that lead to blisters, it hurt circulation. He held the bare foot near the fire, massaging the toes, working them, so that frostbite would not set in. "I apprenticed myself to a chimney sweep. Got too big to get up the chimneys, though. Just as well, chimney sweep boys don't last long—breathing all that coal dust ruins their health. After that, I lived catch as catch can—on the streets, mostly. I done whatever I had to, to get by. I've scavenged garbage heaps, swept streets, had me a root beer stand. I was even a 'resurrection man.' "

Swede scratched his muffler-wrapped jaw. " 'Resurrection man?' "

"Grave robber," Irish Tom explained. Tom was cleaning his rifle, running an oily cloth across the moving surfaces.

"Oh," said Swede in a low voice. He looked at Nails sideways, as though he wondered if Nails had sold his soul to the Devil. After a bit, Swede stretched full length in the snow, letting the sun beat down on him, absorbing what little warmth its rays held. The temperature was below freezing, but there was little wind, so the day was bearable. "I only got two more Christmases in the Army," Swede mused. "When I get out, I'm going home to the farm, and I'm never leaving again."

"Not me," said Tom, squinting down the barrel of his rifle. "I'm openin' a restaurant."

Swede looked over, shielding his eyes from the sun's brilliant glare as it reflected off the snow. He knew how easy it was to come down with snow blindness. "You're going to cook?"

"Nah. I'll hire Chinamen for that."

Swede was puzzled. "You're going to open a Chinese restaurant?"

"Irish restaurant. Chinese cooks. They work cheaper, and they don't back talk you like the damned Irish."

"Christ, that should be a meal to remember. How'd you end up with Uncle Sam's boys in blue, anyway?"

Tom put an oily patch on the end of his ramrod and ran it down the rifle barrel. "When I got to America, there was no jobs to be found, what with the hard times back east, and me bein' Irish. Then one night, I find meself drinking with a fellow, him buyin' and all. I don't recollect much after that, but whin I woke up, there I was with a splittin' headache, and gone for a sojer. I've still no idea how it happened. What's your excuse?"

Swede sat up and tried to make a snowball. The snow still wasn't good. "I wanted to get away from home. See the West, have some adventure. I figured to be a miner, but then the recruiting sergeant come to town. Boy, was he impressive in that blue uniform, with all the girls following him around. I wanted a uniform just like his, and a fine horse just like the one he rode—so I forgot about mining and joined up."

"Horse, eh?" Irish Tom chewed on the word for a bit, then spat in the direction of the bonfire. "Have ye by any chance noticed that ye're in the infantry?"

Swede looked sheepish. "They said there was a mistake with the paperwork. Said I'd be transferred. Reckon it ain't gonna happen now."

Swede and Tom looked at Nails expectantly. He ignored them, smearing pork grease on his foot as protection against blisters and frostbite, then putting his socks back on in the reverse order they'd been on before. They were still looking at him. "All right, if you have to know, it was the middle of winter. I didn't have a cent to my name. I hadn't eaten in days. I was tired of living without a roof over my head, tired of being cold and wet. So I said screw it, and I joined the Army to get warm and get something to eat."

Swede and Irish Tom started laughing. Swede pounded his thighs. Tom fell on his back, dropping his just-cleaned rifle in the snow, but he didn't act like he cared. He was laughing so hard, he was close to tears. "That's a rare one, that is. 'Tis certain you been colder and wetter in the Army than ever you was on the outside."

"You probably ate better when you was scavenging them garbage dumps," Swede added.

When they were done laughing, Tom said, "What are you going to do when you get out?"

"Look you two up and shoot you, for asking so many damn questions."

* * *

After the girl left him, Smith had gone back to his rough society and the rough things he had to do to survive. Books were long forgotten. He'd grown quick with his fists—or with a knife or gun, if it came to that. Last Christmas, he'd killed a man. It wasn't the first man he'd killed, but this one had money and political connections. Smith had gone on the run. He knew this time the hunt wouldn't stop after a few miles or even after a few hundred miles, like it always had before. So he'd joined the Army, to hide. He figured to stay a couple of years, then desert when the storm had blown over.

No chance of that now, he thought.

* * *

The men looked up. The Captain was coming toward them, with the Athlete in tow. The men started to their feet, but the Captain waved them back down. "Merry Christmas, men."

"Merry Christmas, sir," they said.

The Captain crouched beside them. "Join you for coffee?"

"Yes, sir," said Tom. "Our pleasure, sir."

Nails poured coffee in the Captain's cup. The Athlete, who was still standing, hesitated, then held out his cup, and Nails filled it, as well. It was a tradition in the Army for officers to spend time with their men at Christmas. The Captain would visit every mess group this day, and have coffee with each of them. Nails wondered what kept his kidneys from floating away.

"Sorry we can't give you more than coffee, sir," said Irish Tom, grinning.

The Captain grinned back. "So am I." If they were back at the fort, the Captain likely would have shown up with a half-dozen bottles of prime whiskey for their party.

The Captain sipped from his cup. "Good coffee."

"Thank you, sir," said Nails.

The Captain shifted and knelt beside Smith. "How do you feel, Smith?"

Smith lifted his head toward the sound of the voice. He tried to say something. His lips moved, but no words came out.

With his teeth, the Captain pulled off one of his buffalo skin gauntlets and felt Smith's forehead. It was on fire. His breathing was as ragged as his uniform. The Captain put the mitten back on. "Hang in there, son. We'll be back at the fort soon enough."

Smith managed a nod.

"How about you, O'Brian, how are you doing?"

"Grand, sir," said Tom. "Fit as a fiddle." He leaned forward, as if in confidentiality. "Bit peckish, though."

The Captain laughed. "Jernigan—you having a good Christmas?"

"I guess so, sir. Hadn't counted on being quite this cold."

"Helps you get in the spirit," the Captain told him. "What about you, Morrison—you doing all right?"

"I always do all right, sir," Nails said.

The Captain chatted with the men for a bit. Tom and Swede talked readily enough; Nails kept quiet, occasionally bathing Smith's hot forehead with snow. They could never be this informal at the fort. There, the men could only speak to an officer with the First Sergeant's permission, and that was given rarely. At last the Captain rose. "I'll be back to check on Smith later."

"Yes, sir," said the three men.

"Thanks for the coffee."

"Yes," added the Athlete, who was still standing. "Thanks."

* * *

Before visiting the next mess, the Captain motioned the Lieutenant out of the men's earshot. The Captain was a rangy fellow, with a gravelly voice. He'd been a colonel during the war, but unless another big war came along, or a lot of his superiors got killed by the Indians, a captain was all he was ever going to be. He could have ridden a horse on the scout but didn't, preferring to walk like the men. Partly, this was to share the men's hardship, partly to avoid bringing along more pack mules. This had forced the Lieutenant—who would have preferred to ride—to walk, as well.

The Captain said, "You all right, Owen? You didn't say a word back there."

The Lieutenant sighed. "I know, sir, but I couldn't think of anything to say. I don't think I'm cut out for this. At home right now, I'd be heading for a fancy dress ball. Here I am, half starving in a snowdrift. I feel out of place here. I feel like I don't belong."

"That's to be expected. You've only been with the company a short time."

The Lieutenant said, "I envy you, sir—your way with the men. They like you, but they respect you at the same time. They don't feel that way about me."

"That kind of respect doesn't come overnight."

"I don't think it will ever come to me."

"What are you saying?"

"I—I'm thinking of resigning my commission."

"I see. Well, it's your decision. Just don't be too hasty. Give the Army a chance."

"Be honest, sir—do you think I've the makings of a good officer?"

The Captain cocked his head. "Maybe, but there's only one way to find out for sure."

They moved on to the next fire.

* * *

The hunters came back. They had found no game. "Blizzard's drove everything to ground," said Fitzpatrick, the civilian scout.

The men, who had gathered around in anticipation, went back to their fires, disappointed. "Jayus, I was hopin' they'd come up with somethin'," said Tom.

"A turkey, maybe," said Big Abner.

"A buffalo," said Horsethief Hinkle.

"Hell, I'd have been happy with a rabbit," said Ben the Walrus. Ben had gotten his nickname from his appearance when he enlisted. Two years of Army food and about a thousand miles of marching had slimmed him down considerably.

Tom rubbed his gloved hands together. "Looks like we'll have to make do with what's in the pantry."

* * *

Already on this short day the sun had passed its zenith. It was sinking into the west, losing what little heat it had brought. The crust of the snow, which had turned slushy, started to harden again as the boys got ready for their Christmas dinner. The Captain had a couple of onions. These were fried and carefully divided in equal amounts among the eight mess groups. The First Sergeant had a large potato, which was likewise parceled out. The Athlete opened a couple tins of peaches from his pack. Each man got a spoonful of the heavy syrup—Smith first—then they ate the peaches as an appetizer. They boiled more coffee and built up their cook fires.

Irish Tom had managed to save a bit of vinegar, some of which he traded to Ben the Walrus for a chunk of brown sugar. Welsh Willie lent him four raisins. Tom soaked the hardtack in melted snow. The salt pork was green with age, the fat hanging off it. Tom scraped off ancient mouse droppings, then soaked the pork in the vinegar. When the tack had absorbed enough water to bring it to a consistency softer than rock, Tom wrapped it in his bandanna and hammered it to pieces with the butt of his bowie knife. He sliced the vinegar-soaked pork into cubes and fried them in his field pan. When the fat was rendered sufficiently, he added the drained hardtack bits, and their tiny piece of the First Sergeant's potato, cut in four. He stirred the mixture in the sizzling grease. When it was just about cooked, he added the four raisins, to plump them, then folded in the precious onions. For a finish, he crushed the sugar and sprinkled it across the meal's top. He scooped an exact quarter of the mixture in each man's mess kit, topping each serving with one of the plumped raisins.

"There you are, lads. As grand a Christmas feast as you're ever like to see. All it wants is a drop of whiskey to wash it down."

Nails averted his gaze. He didn't know why—he didn't feel guilty about the brandy. No one had ever shared with him. No one had ever given him a thing. They said he was a hard case—well, he was.

Around them, the other mess groups were eating. The ingredients were by and large the same, their preparation limited only by the cooks' imaginations. Some of the men took their time, savoring each bite, others shoveled the food into their mouths. Nails fed Smith again, forcing the food into him, resentful of every bite the dying man took.

When it came his own turn, Nails ate the raisin,

the onions and the morsel of potato. When that was done, he found that he wasn't all that hungry. Salt pork—what did he care about salt pork when he had brandy? The pork was barely recognizable as food. Most dogs would turn up their noses at it, but the saps around him went at it like it was prime beef or Smithfield ham. Nails took the salt pork from his mess tin. He wrapped it in his handkerchief and stuck it in his coat pocket. Maybe later. It was time for him to go on guard. He hefted his rifle and trudged off to his spot on the company perimeter.

* * *

The light began to fade. The sun turned into a dull red ball, low on the western horizon. The soft rosy glow that it cast on the sky spread across the frozen landscape, giving the scene a bleak beauty. One of the boys broke out a penny whistle. Another had a Jew's harp. They stood by the bonfire and began playing "Hark, the Herald Angels Sing." The playing was ragged at first, then got better. Clatterbuck the trumpeter joined in, lending a brass accompaniment. A few of the boys started to sing along, then more.

* * *

The Captain sat in the snow by his tent, writing a letter to his wife, Elizabeth. There was no chance of the letter being delivered before they got back to the fort, but he did it nonetheless. It made him feel like Elizabeth was here with him—in spirit, at least. He wondered what she had done today. Gone sleigh riding, he guessed, using the sleighs they'd built from packing crates, the officers falling all over themselves trying to be deferential to the ladies, especially the Colonel's wife. The Captain's mouth turned up at the thought of that old battle axe being fussed over by handsome young lieutenants. Elizabeth would be taking Christmas dinner with Major Crawford and his wife. Later, there would be a ball at the commanding officer's quarters. The other officers would make sure that Elizabeth never missed a dance.

The singing grew louder as more of the men joined in. The Captain sighed. He and his wife had buried three children at various posts on the frontier. There was no chance of more children. His wife had given up everything she had ever wanted for his career, and here, on the most important day of the year, he couldn't be there for her.

He licked his pencil and wrote in his orderly book:

"My Dearest Elizabeth,

Here it is, Christmas, and once again we are apart. I wish with all my heart that it could not be so, but I know you will be in good hands with Annie and Tim Crawford.

The sun made an appearance today. The temperature rose above zero for the first time in several days. Right now it is dusk, clear and cold, as it must have been on that first Christmas night. The men are singing. They seem cheerful enough. All in all, a comforting scene.

I wish I could be there to give you my gift. But what can I give you, who have given me everything? What can I give you that would ever match the magnitude of your sacrifice for me? I took your comfortable life and turned it into one of hardship and sorrow, yet you never complained. I owe you so much, and all I can give you is my love . . .

Did you go to the cemetery today? I am sure that you did. I so wish I could have been with you, to . . ."

* * *

He let out his breath and stopped writing. He couldn't go on.

The First Sergeant saw him. "You all right, sir?"

The Captain closed his orderly book. "Yes, fine." He smacked his palms on his knees and stood. "Let's join the singing, shall we?"

As the Captain tucked the orderly book into his greatcoat, the First Sergeant saw the Athlete sitting dejected, with his head on his fists. "You, too, sir. Come along." The First could use this chivvying tone with a mere lieutenant; he would never have tried it with the Captain.

The Athlete looked up, surprised. "What?"

"The singing, sir."

The Athlete's youthful face brightened. "Oh. Yes. Of course." He followed the Captain and the First Sergeant to the fire.

* * *

The entire company was gathered around the bonfire now. Even the Athlete had overcome his initial reticence and was singing as lustily as any of them—"See Amid the Winter's Snow," "It Came Upon the Midnight Clear." Irish Tom and the Swede held Smith upright between them. It had gone dark. The firelight reflected off the brass belt buckles and the bayonet on the tree, making the tree shimmer with light in the breeze, making it seem alive.

* * *

Smith listened to the massed voices. He wanted to sing with them, but he was too weak. He wished he could be a boy once more, helping his father bring the tree inside, with the chill wind blowing, and his mother red faced from baking, and his sister laughing in glee at the size of the new-cut tree . . .

* * *

The Swede nudged Irish Tom. With his head he indicated Smith. Tears were running down Smith's cheeks.

* * *

Smith wanted to say a prayer. He couldn't remember any, so he made up his own. "Please, God, forgive me. I'm sorry for all I've done. I've made mistakes. I've made a lot of them. I'd change them if I could, but I can't. I never meant to hurt anybody. Please forgive me."

* * *

Nails was off by himself, on guard. He slipped the pint of brandy from his pocket and sighed. He'd been waiting for this all day. He uncorked the bottle, licking his lips. The men were singing "God Rest Ye Merry, Gentlemen." Roaring it, their sturdy voices rising as one into the snowbound night:

> *"God rest ye merry, gentlemen.*
> *Let nothing you dismay.*
> *Remember Christ our Savior*
> *Was born on Christmas Day,*

To save us all from Satan's Pow'r
When we were gone astray.

Oh, tidings of comfort and joy,
Comfort and joy.
Oh, tidings of comfort and joy."

Nails waited with the bottle, listening as they went through two more verses, the voices crescendoing at the end:

"Oh, tidings of comfort and joy."

Suddenly—silence. Echoes floated across the prairie. That was the end; the musicians had played all the Christmas songs they knew. Nails put the bottle to his lips.

Then a lone voice sounded out in German:

"Stille nacht, heilige Nacht,
Alles schlaft, einsam wacht . . . "

Nails stopped, listening once more. It was a simple hymn, all the more beautiful because of its simplicity. None of the boys knew German, but some of them began to hum along, then all of them.

Nails found himself humming, too. The cold was forgotten and the weariness.

"Home . . ." "Family . . ."

This *was* his home, Nails realized. This *was* his family. This was a place he could belong, if he'd let himself.

He corked the bottle and stuck it back in his coat.

When Nails came off guard, he returned to his mess fire, where the boys were preparing for tattoo. Smitty was there, propped against their packs, looking oddly rested. Nails sat beside him. He tapped Smitty's shoulder. Smitty looked over. Nails offered him the bottle. Smitty's fevered eyes questioned him—*"Why?"*

Nails hesitated. This was hard for him to do. He shrugged and, in a low voice, said, "Merry Christmas."

Smitty gave a faint nod.

Nails held the back of Smitty's head. He tilted the bottle to the dying man's lips. Smitty swallowed, coughed, bent over.

"More?" Nails said.

Smitty nodded again.

Nails gave him another drink. Another. Then Smitty shook his head. He'd had enough. He closed his eyes.

Nails saw Tom and Swede eyeing him. "Where'd you come by the bottle?" Tom asked.

"Found it. Out there."

They knew he was lying, of course, but they didn't say anything. Nails handed them the bottle. Each took a long pull, then they offered it back. Nails waved them off. "My Christmas present," he told them.

They drank some more, then Tom said, "I've misjudged ye, Nails. Ye're all right."

No one had ever said that to him before.

The Swede grinned broadly. "Hey—maybe this is our Christmas miracle."

"Aye," said Tom. "Maybe 'tis, at that."

Tom and the Swede passed the bottle back and forth. They saved the last drink for Smitty. Right after that, the Captain came to their fire. He must have smelled the alcohol, but he said nothing. He knelt beside Smith. Smith's forehead was no longer hot. It was clammy now; his breathing sounded like pebbles rolling across a tin washboard. "Is there anything you want to tell me, son?" the Captain asked.

* * *

Smith looked up. Odd—it was summer. The hot sun beat down. "I . . . I . . . " His hand clawed the Captain's coat sleeve. He had to make him understand. "I had a . . . sister . . . "

"Her name, man—her name."

But it didn't matter, because there she was. She was standing beneath the old shade tree, waving to him, beckoning him to join her as she had done so many times before.
He went to her.

* * *

Gently, the Captain released the dead man's grip. He laid Smith on the snow. With his thumb he closed Smith's sightless eyes. Then he hung his head. "Somewhere, there's someone who'd like to know what happened to him. We'll never be able to tell them. We don't even know his real name."

"He must have gone out happy," said the Swede. "He looks real peaceful."

"Look at the smile on his face," marveled Tom. "I never seen him smile before."

* * *

The next day, Smith was buried and the march resumed. The men fell into line and slogged through the snow, past Smith's grave, past their tree, now stripped of its ornaments. Another one of the men had fallen ill, and the Athlete carried his pack. Nails marched alongside Irish Tom and the Swede. As the First Sergeant cursed them and told them to pick up the pace, Nails stuck his hands in his coat pockets. There he found the salt pork from the night before. He unwrapped it and took a bite.

He had never tasted anything so good in his life.

For our goodbye story, Paul Sekulich encapsulates the feelings of all the contributors to this anthology.

THE DOOMED LIFE OF BILLY CAVANAUGH

By Paul Sekulich

Billy Cavanaugh knew the Kodiak bear that faced him a mere six feet away was how he was going to die. It stood nine feet tall on its hind legs, its huge claws raised like a hairy percussionist ready to crush out his life between two enormous meat cymbals. Retreating was impossible. His kid brother, Dougie, was clinging to him, plastered to his back, thrashing and muttering incoherently like an entranced voodoo dancer. This was the end. Might as well face up to it, this would be his last summer. He was never going to see his dog Foot-Foot again, and that bear was going to eat every morsel of him. There wouldn't even be a pinky bone left to bury. Billy also knew he was never going to see thirteen, or that cute Darlene Bateman in eighth grade homeroom.

"You fellas are going to miss feeding the sea lions at the next exhibit if you don't hurry," the zoo guide said.

"Okay," Billy said, and he piggy-backed Dougie out of the bear diorama.

Minutes later, the two brothers were tossing sardines to the sea lions in the water arena. Billy knew that as soon as he ran out of sardines the huge male, who was eyeing him, would dive across the retainer wall and start gnawing on his throat with those three-inch fangs. He doled out the last of the sardines frugally, then slinked his way toward the concession stand. Once there, he could get more stuff to feed the big bruiser, or hide in a Port-A-Potty and wait him out.

Sidling away from the arena by shifting his feet from side to side brought him abruptly against a woman holding a canvas souvenir bag and a cup of lemonade.

"Where do you think you're going, young man?" she said.

"Oh, hi, Mom," Billy said. "Just thought I'd head over to the snack bar. Could use a stiff drink."

"Want a sip of my stiff lemonade?" his mother asked.

"Mom, please. I'm twelve. Don't embarrass me."

"It's a sip of lemonade. It's not like I'm going to breast feed you."

Billy needed to make a decision: Stay for more family humiliation or bolt for the concession stand and take his chances with the earless carnivore.

He bolted.

At the soda stand he looked back at the water arena. He'd lucked out. The big sea lion had decided to mooch sardines off a fat guy in the crowd who had bought three buckets of the feed fish. Billy felt like he'd dodged a slick, 600-pound, furry torpedo.

While Billy waited for his root beer, he remembered that things always came in threes for some strange reason, like the Three Musketeers, the Three Stooges, and triple dog dares. Not always good things either. He wondered where the next menace in this unstoppable cycle would pop up to snuff out his life.

Billy caught a glimpse of the man making his

root beer put something weird in his drink. *Is he trying to poison me?* Billy paid the man, took his soda, and carefully examined the contents of the quart-size, Super Swig cup. Suspicions confirmed. There was a curious slice of lemon floating atop the crushed ice. *What? Did the dolt think I'd ordered iced tea? Who puts lemon slices in root beer?* Well, it wasn't cyanide, but that just meant that the third evil in the "curse of threes" was still waiting in the wings for him, like that Mr. Death guy in the *Final Destination* movies.

Late that night, Billy lay in his twin bed across the room from Dougie, who slept peacefully, oblivious to the dangers in the room as he soaked his Star Trek pillow with a steady ooze of drool. Mr. Spock's pointy left ear was getting the worst of it. At that very moment, Billy spotted a spider web in the corner of the ceiling above his bed. He knew it was filled with peril. The black widow that lived there could tiptoe down the wall behind his headboard and bite him right on his neck for maximum effect. Then she'd carry over her young to feast on his tender, pre-teen, paralyzed flesh.

Then there was that 8-foot black cobra that lay coiled under his bed, waiting for the perfect moment to slither up the mattress and fang-dangle him on his exposed leg. Billy had read in school that cobras were the slowest striking of all the known poisonous snakes, but he'd also read that they were still way faster than 20,000 Polynesian natives last year.

Sleep finally arrived, but Billy's dreams were filled with macabre scenes that Louis Carroll never thought of for Alice and the dangers lurking in that rabbit hole.

The next morning, Billy's mother informed him that she had arranged for him to take some aptitude tests being offered at his middle school. *Doesn't she know it's summer? You don't send a kid to school in summer.* It was like going to the chair in those old gangster movies. Or worse, like in *The Green Mile* where that guy with the pet mouse was strapped in and got zapped with about a scazillion volts without his head sponge getting properly water-soaked. The man actually caught *on fire* in the scene, and with it, the horrific images Billy witnessed were indelibly burned into his brain.

He always felt sorry for kids who had to take remedial classes in summer school, and equated it with being sent to one of those French penal colonies like he'd seen in *Papillion.*

"It'll help us decide which colleges will be best for you when you graduate," Billy's mother said.

"Mom, college is a hundred years away. I'm twelve."

"You'll be eighteen before you know it. So get dressed. We have to be there in an hour."

Wait a minute, Billy thought. *The test's at school . . . in the summer, no less. That's it. That's the third evil thing. And boy, it's right up there with a visit from Mr. Death.*

After the tests, Mrs. Cavanaugh sat down in a closed office with the test proctors and the psychologists who specialized in evaluating occupational aptitude test results. Billy sat outside, out of earshot, but he knew what was going on in there. They were scrutinizing his report cards and his just-barely-okay grades, but it was those teacher comments that were going to sink him. Things like, "He daydreams a lot and stares out the window when he should be paying attention," or "He doesn't follow directions," or, his personal favorite, "He seems to live in a world of his own."

Billy knew those tests would never reveal that he'd be an excellent scuba diver for Spanish treasures off the coast of Florida, or that he would make a super NASCAR driver, certain to win the Daytona 500 in record time. Those tests would come back showing what a terrific used car salesman he'd make or, worse, a plumber. He also knew those tests were loaded with trick questions that you had to be on guard for, like that one about the sunrise. "The sun rises in the: a) north, b) east, c) south, d) west (circle one)." All the time he knew they were messing with him, so he wrote in the correct answer: *morning.*

The door of the office opened and out walked the test sadists and his mother. His mom approached, looking like the veterinarian who is about to tell you your guppy didn't make it. She handed Billy a piece of paper and puckered a tiny, hurt-looking smile.

Billy read the paper and almost fell out of his chair. It was worse than he ever imagined. It would mean living in torment for the rest of his days. He was doomed. *Please make sure my head sponge is really, really wet.*

The paper said that he was most suited to be a fiction writer.

CURTAIN CALL

ALAN AMRHINE — I was born in, and write from, the city in which Poe died — Baltimore, Maryland. Okay, so maybe that's the only similarity. But when fog sifts in from the harbor and lies wet on the cobblestone streets; when that dampness and denseness of air seems to magnify every sound — why, there is no doubt his blood runs beneath these streets. It's the beating of the old man's heart we hear, and there will always be stories to tell.

Other influences include Shirley Jackson, Ray Bradbury, Stephen King, Dylan Thomas, H.P. Lovecraft, Mark Twain, Dean Koontz, T.S. Eliot, Jack London and Harlan Ellison. Also Rod Serling's *Twilight Zone*. I won't mention the ones that would make this list really eclectic. Special thanks to Robert Broomall, Joya Fields and Kraft Rompf — three Maryland authors: two novelists and a poet — who have been mentors and beacons in my life.

I hope you enjoy the stories. After all, that's what it's all about. Well, that and the "Hokey Pokey."

AMY BOCK — Although she grew up in Belgium, Amy Bock has lived in Harford County, Maryland, for 18 years. She is a graduate of Notre Dame of Maryland University, where she majored in English and was an editor for *Damozel*, the campus literary magazine. Amy currently works for a family business in Bel Air, Maryland.

ROBERT BROOMALL — For as long as I can remember, I've wanted to be a writer. I was one of those kids who always had his nose stuck in a book. My head was full of exotic characters and places and events, and my dream was to be able to create stories like the ones I read. Now that I actually am a writer, I sometimes can't believe it's happened. It seems like it was someone else who wrote those books. Either way, it's a dream come true.

Influences? C.S. Forester (the one and only), Robert Louis Stevenson, Agatha Christie, and others too numerous to mention. Contemporary influences — the late, great George MacDonald Fraser and Bernard Cornwell.

Robert Broomall is the author of sixteen novels. His most recent, Death's Head: A Tale of the Third Crusade, *is currently being serialized on Amazon.com, and will be completed in early 2016.*

SHARON BROOMALL — I spent most of my young life pretending I didn't want to be a writer. That may sound strange coming from someone who has made a living as a writer and editor for more than two decades. For me it was a struggle to find my voice, and realizing I have the vision to paint a picture no one else can paint.

I don't have literary influences per se; musicians have inspired my writing as much as other writers. I believe my best writing happens when I stay true to my characters and to myself. Authors whose work I enjoy and admire include Jim Benton (*Dear Dumb Diary*), John Irving, John Updike, Diana Gabaldon, Emily Dickinson, and Sue Grafton.

Photography is another of my passions, and another medium for my vision. A gallery of my work is now online at *sharonbroomallphotographer.com.*

Sharon Broomall is the author of Gabby Gibson: Middle School Detective, *available from Blue Stone.*

T. L. EMERY — Terry Emery's writing has been influenced by his literary idols Stephen King, Neil Gaiman, and Ray Bradbury. As such most of his work has something of the fantastic in it. He's a fan of horror, fantasy, and magical realism. He is currently working on a novella centered in his fictional universe of Hill County, West Virginia.

CHARLES GODFREY — Charles K. Godfrey began his career in the Baltimore County Fire Department as a firefighter and was quickly promoted to paramedic. He was promoted to lieutenant and served in the Fire Investigation Division. He retired as a Fire Lieutenant with 27 years' service.

During this time, he joined the First Maryland Volunteer Infantry Regiment as a reenactor. For more than twenty years, he participated in the reenactments of Gettysburg, Manassas, Cedar Creek, and many other battles, as well as living history events at Fort McHenry and Harpers Ferry. He participated in the 150th anniversary ceremonies at Gettysburg. He is a history buff who likes to blend fiction with history. In addition, he is enthusiastic about science fiction and loves the idea of time travel. He resides in northern Baltimore County with his wife of 40 years.

Charles Godfrey is the author of the alternate history thriller The Final Charge *and the recently published sequel,* The Death Machine.

KEITH HOSKINS — Keith J. Hoskins is a short story author, and award-winning poet. He is currently working on his first novel: *Kray and the Coveted Seer,* a fantasy novel set in a magical world. Keith's main genres of interest are fantasy, science fiction, and thrillers. When he's not fighting off dragons or piloting a spaceship through an asteroid belt, he's most likely spending quality time at home with his wife Donna, his son Bailey, and their mischievous schnauzer, Harley.

BOB KNAPP — Now leaning toward the elderly side of life, Bob Knapp, in addition to writing, has welcomed several challenges: The Great Courses, singing in his church's choir, and the ukulele. His first published fictional work was a novel, *The Devil's Palm.* Material for his stories often comes from his long ago past, as is true for the short story "The House," included in this anthology. Bob resides with his wife and five family members in Perry Hall, Maryland.

JOE LONG — I'm compelled to write. Worlds and characters and adventures pour out of my head and I catch as much of it on paper as I can. I love fantasy and science and the worlds they can build, both subtle and fantastic. I love word craft, making the ugly sound beautiful, and the beautiful sound magical. My inspirations are Asimov, Barker, Herbert and cummings, and all the wonderful places they've taken me.

PAUL SEKULICH — Paul has lived in New York, Detroit, Chicago; Stuart and Palm Beach, Florida; Manhattan Beach, Los Angeles and Hollywood, California. He holds a B.A. in Theatre from the University of Maryland and Masters of Fine Arts credits from Towson University and the University of Southern California.

Paul is a member of the Screen Actors Guild, The American Federation of Television & Radio Artists, and the Actors Equity Association. As a former professor of theatre, he has directed numerous college productions and taught acting, directing and scriptwriting. In Hollywood he worked as a script doctor for two prime time television comedies.

He has written, acted in, produced and directed films, commercials and stage productions since he was 18 and has won awards for his work. He owned and operated The Limestone Dinner Theatre for several years and now tours the country teaching seminars on screenwriting for television and the movies.

Paul lives with his wife Joyce in Maryland.

Paul Sekulich is the author of the thrillers The Omega Formula, A Killer Season and Island of Last Resort. *His next book,* Deep Death, *will be available soon.*

MARK LEE TAYLOR — Mark Lee Taylor published his first novel, *A Pebble Tossed*, in 2014, and is currently working on his second. He grew up in Harford County, Maryland, and still lives there with his wife, teenage daughter, and two dogs. He still doesn't have a smartphone, but he never goes anywhere without his iPod, and his wildly eclectic music library could play for 146 days without repeating a song. If he could, he would spend the rest of his life writing and snorkeling in the Caribbean, but not at the same time.

CHRIS VAUGHAN — Christopher J. Vaughan has been writing since the third grade, although much of that early work has fallen into obscurity. He writes in several genres, but he's most least known for his science-fiction stories. His *Lara: Queen of the Rocket People* (which marked Parker Wiley's first appearance) is widely acclaimed.*

Chris lives in Finksburg, Maryland, with his wife, dog, and more toys than any man should be allowed to have.

* As an excellent way to fix wobbly tables.